The LOVE
We Almost
LOST

Russell F. Moran

The Love We Almost Lost

Coddington Press

Copyright © 2020 by Russell F. Moran

www.morancom.com

Printed in the United States of America

ISBN: 978-1-7338872-6-7

Covers and text design by LuAnn T. Palazzo
www.TheDesignDiva.net

DEDICATION

This book is dedicated to tthe medical research scientists of the world.

ACKNOWLEDGEMENTS

As always, I thank my wife, Lynda, for her attentive reading, rereading, and editing of my many drafts, and for laughing at my jokes. Lynda is to me as Becca is to Jack. Lynda makes a cameo appearance in this book. I also thank my friend and editor, John White, for his keen editorial eye. John and his dog, Chico, make a cameo appearance in the book. I thank LuAnn T. Palazzo for her expert interior and cover designs. And I especially thank my readers, many of whom are a constant source of inspiration and encouragement for me.

AUTHOR'S NOTE

The Love We Almost Lost a love story and a terrorist thriller. It is the story of Navy physician Rebecca (Becca) Lang and her husband, FBI Agent and former Marine Captain, Jack Parker. Becca and Jack are two of my favorite characters, and I think of them as old friends. As I wrote this book, we took a lot of adventures together. I hope you will see them that way too.

You will find a **Cast of Characters** after the last chapter of the book. It can be frustrating to come across a character on page 150, that you first met on page 20, especially if you've put the book down for a few days. I've seen this done in Russian literature, and I happily add a cast of characters to *The Love We Almost Lost* as well as my other novels.

Chapter 1

A military hospital in Afghanistan is an unlikely place to find romance. But you don't always get to plan things your way during a war.

It's stupid for a doctor to be romantically involved with a patient under her care. In the United States Armed Forces it's worse because it violates regulations. The reason it's stupid is because a doctor needs to remain clinical and dispassionate. If you have strong personal feelings for a patient, your sensitivity can interfere with your objectivity.

But Marine Captain John Parker made me stupid. A platoon leader, he had been seriously injured in a firefight just outside the city of Bagram, Afghanistan, the location of Bagram Airfield. I had been "in country" for only five days and was assigned to combat surgery duty as a Navy Lieutenant at the Craig Joint Theater Hospital located at the airfield. The 50-bed hospital was completely modern, as impressive as any hospital I'd seen in the U.S. The U.S. military expects a lot from its people and gives back in exchange. When Captain Parker was carried into the hospital, I could immediately see that he suffered a bad shoulder wound from gunfire. He was bleeding profusely. There's a common misconception that combat surgeons operate on the "stitch in time" rule. Just do what you can and do it fast. Well, that's partially true, but only partially. Yes, you do need to move fast, but you also need to move accurately. No sense racing across the finish line only to discover that the line consists of your patient's dead body. It's important to remain calm and apply every bit of skill you have. Whether you're treating a soldier or Marine wounded in combat or attending a car accident victim in a civilian hospital in the States, it's up to you the doctor to give that patient your best. It can be the difference between life and death. I know that sounds dramatic but it's the truth.

My first task with Captain Parker's shoulder wound was to slow down the bleeding, which I did with a pressure point tourniquet. If I didn't stop the bleeding, I could lose him. This brave Marine needed my help and I was there to give it to him. He had lost an enormous amount of blood and I was concerned that he might not make it. I ordered a transfusion from our blood bank. Thank God he didn't have a rare blood type. After the bleeding stopped, I had to work on his entry and exit wounds. I was happy to observe that the bullet mercifully passed through soft tissue, without destroying any skeletal structure. It was a low caliber bullet, one designed for accuracy, and didn't damage too much muscle tissue. After debriding his wounds and suturing him, I placed him in critical condition. From the report I read, he was shot as he stood his ground firing at enemy soldiers who converged on his platoon. Pretty courageous if you ask me. He was in obvious pain, too weak to talk, and breathing heavily.

The hospital was busy that day with 20 newly admitted soldiers and Marines suffering from various injuries, mainly bullet wounds. Keeping the hospital from turning into chaos was up to me and the rest of the medical staff. We keep reminding ourselves that we're on a military base subject to attack as it had been last year by local Taliban insurgents.

It takes a special kind of lowlife to attack a hospital, and Afghanistan had plenty of lowlifes. That afternoon I stopped by to check up on Captain Parker, as I found myself doing more and more often. He was my first combat surgery patient and I wanted to make sure everything was okay. He was one tough guy, and he was making an amazing recovery. When I walked up to his bed he was actually sitting up and talking to an attendant. The duty physician had upgraded his condition from critical to fair. When the captain saw me, he broke out into a big smile. Wow, that smile is beautiful. Come to think of it, everything about him is beautiful, except for his left shoulder. He remembered my treating him earlier, which surprised me because he was semi-conscious at the time. His complexion was good, nothing like the pallor of earlier, and his breathing was normal. Not only was his complexion good, it was breathtaking. My God, what a handsome guy. He stared into my eyes, which made me dizzy for some strange reason. What the hell is going on with me? Hey, I'm a doctor doing my rounds.

"Nice to see you again, Lieutenant Lang," he said.

"Please call me Becca." I seemed to have misplaced my regulations manual.

"And call me Jack." He lost his as well.

"You're one talented surgeon, Becca. My shoulder still hurts, but nothing like this morning."

He never took his eyes off me, and I liked that—a lot. Maybe too much?

"I'm glad to hear that, Captain Jack. Keeping your shoulder immobile is important. The good news is that the bullet went through the soft tissue of your shoulder without causing too much damage. With a lot of physical therapy, you should fully recover, although you will have a lot of pain for a while."

"Will you help me recover, Becca?"

"I certainly will, it's my job."

"Then we should go out on a date. I feel better already just thinking about it."

"Hey, wiseguy, I don't date men with bullet holes." He had a cute sense of humor and I enjoyed joking with him.

"Well, I no longer have bullet holes thanks to you, so I'll take that as an acceptance of my date offer."

"Captain Jack, are you flirting with me?"

"Yes, I'm afraid I am. Do you mind?" He wrapped those goddam beautiful ocean blue eyes around me.

"No, I don't mind." I should have cut it off right there, but sometimes what I *should* do doesn't line up with what I *want to do*. And what I want to do has nothing to do with my work as a Navy doctor. Not one bit. I shouldn't feel attracted to a patient, but how do I tell that to my pounding heart. Besides his good looks he had a warm, pleasant, genuine way about him. I think my mom, with her perceptive take on human nature, would call a man like him, "the real deal." I had just operated on this guy and something inside me said to keep on operating. *Hey, slow down, take a deep breath.*

"May I ask you a question, Becca, but on a different subject."

"Of course. Part of my job is to answer questions."

"Are you always this beautiful or does it have something to do with the medicine I'm taking?"

"You are definitely a flirt, Captain Jack. I'll be back shortly,"

I said, patting his good shoulder. "I expect to hear some more unique flirting lines." I was trying for some awkward humor. I wanted to tell him that flirting will get him nowhere.

But I'd be lying.

"You have my promise," he said, flashing that damn cute smile. "I'll have some great flirtations for you the next time you come by."

"I look forward to hearing them."

I had plenty of rounds to perform that day, but something told me to keep rounding up on Captain Jack. Every few minutes I would return to his bedside and we'd continue the conversation we had started earlier.

"You look familiar, Doc. Do you come here often?"

"If that's your best flirting line, Captain, you have some work ahead of you."

He cracked up, but suddenly winced from the pain in his shoulder. Laughter and injuries don't go together well. I rearranged his pillow to take the pressure off his shoulder. I went lightly on his pain medications with his full agreement. We both wanted him to avoid getting addicted to painkillers, as too often happens with serious injuries. As I said, he's one tough guy both physically and emotionally. It's easy to admire a man like him. I sure as hell did and not just because of his sweet personality and drop-dead gorgeous looks. Well, I'm sure that had something to do with it. Okay, a lot to do with it. To help with his pain, I decided to teach him some meditation exercises. One of my favorites, and the most successful, requires the patient to imagine that his wound has size, color, and shape, and to keep letting the changing images into his mind. This technique focuses your attention, and, amazingly, lessens the pain. You would think that the objective of the exercise should be to take your mind off the pain, but the thinking behind this Eastern medicine exercise is to engage your mind with the pain, and miraculously it disappears. Something about fully experiencing the pain, not trying to deny it. I'm not sure I understand it, but I've seen it work many times. A couple of years ago I sprained an ankle playing tennis, and it hurt like a bitch. I tried the meditation process and the pain went away. That sold me on the technique.

"Now listen, Captain Jack. We're going to go through a meditation exercise that should help with your pain. It's important that you just answer my questions without analyzing or editing your answers. Okay, here goes. "What color is your shoulder pain?"

"What do you mean, what color? I don't understand the question."

"Hey, remember the rules. No analyzing and no editing my questions. Now, again, what color is your shoulder pain?"

"It's red."

"Now, what shape is it?"

"What?"

"Hey, no analyzing."

"Okay, it's shaped like a pineapple."

"And how much does your shoulder pain weigh?"

"Fifty pounds."

I went through a dozen of these three-part questions, each time asking him what color, shape, and weight of his shoulder pain. The whole process took less than 10 minutes.

"Okay, so how does your shoulder feel now?"

"I can't believe this, Becca, but the pain is gone. It's like I was never wounded. Are you a doctor or a magician?"

"I'm a doctor who doesn't hesitate to use different techniques, some of which aren't from Western medicine. Your pain will return, and when it does, just go through the exercise we just did. I'll do it with you if you like."

"Yes, I'd prefer that you do it with me."

"But they're just a string of questions. You can ask them yourself."

"Yeah, but if you do the asking, I'll get to spend more time with you."

"Hey, Captain Jack, you are one definite flirty bird."

"I'll admit that I am, and something tells me you kind of like it."

Yes, I do like his flirting, but I didn't tell him so, of course. His sweet flirts made me feel close to him. What the hell is going on with me?

He reacted well with the meditation exercise and his pain definitely subsided. It's a wonderful feeling when you can help alleviate suffering without drugs. Making him feel better made me feel better, as it should between doctor and patient. But my feelings toward him went a lot further than the usual doctor-patient stuff. A lot further. *Oh boy.*

We talked nonstop about everything and I felt like I'd known him forever. As a diligent doctor, I researched his personal file. Wow, this guy is no slouch. He graduated at the top of his class at Columbia University and even wrote a book in his senior year. The book, *Desert Memories*, almost hit *The New York Times* best seller list. It was a story about the wartime travails of a Marine officer, written in anticipation of his service, no doubt. I was impressed not only by his excellent writing but by his scholarly research into the Marine Corps and military life in general. I found myself using the book as a reference document to orient my head to my military surroundings. I recommended it to my colleagues, most of whom loved it.

The action that got him wounded secured his place as a genuine hero. Not only did he receive the Purple Heart for his injury, he was awarded the Distinguished Service Cross, an advanced decoration for valor. Like I said, he's no slouch. And he's got a great sense of humor. And he's pleasant to talk to. And he's insanely gorgeous. Oh, my goodness, I think I'm really starting to like this guy.

During my visits, to emphasize a point, Captain Jack would occasionally reach over and squeeze my hand. More and more often I found myself squeezing back. Once, when he let go of my hand, I said, "Hey, what's that about?"

"I'm sorry, I just like to hold your hand," he said.

"So why did you let go? Please put your hand in mine again. It's a nice feeling."

Oh, my God, did I just say that? What the hell was going on? I really didn't know, but something was definitely happening. And I liked what was happening. *Holy shit, I don't think I learned this in medical school.*

A week later I diligently walked into the field hospital to check up on Jack. I no longer call him Captain Parker or Captain Jack. No, he's Jack, friendly, pleasant, gorgeous Jack. I found myself checking up on him often— quite often. Hey,

I'm a caring doctor. Taking care of patients is my job.

Right?

But suddenly my feet stopped, unable to move. He was hugging a tall beautiful blond. What the hell is that all about? I made a quick left, stopped to check the pulse of another patient, and beat a hasty retreat out the side door. I'm not a kid, but suddenly I felt like a broken-hearted teenager. Hey, time to snap out of it. He's my patient, not my boyfriend.

Later that day I stopped by to see Jack, being careful to make sure there were no beautiful women nearby.

Judging from the big smile on his face, he seemed happy to see me. I stood next to his bed, struggling valiantly to appear calm, which wasn't easy. I was on a mission—to find out who the hell that blond was.

"I missed you this morning," he said. "I've grown accustomed to your visits. I think I saw you in the distance."

"I saw you too, but I didn't want to interrupt your meeting with that pretty blond."

There, I got it on the table. My heart was pounding out of my chest waiting for his response.

"That was Rachel. I really wanted you to meet her, but you took off."

"You two seemed to be quite close, and I didn't want to interfere," my wiseass mouth snapped.

"Yes, we're very close. Rachel's my good buddy. She's also my favorite sister."

Praise Jesus! It would have been embarrassing to do a cartwheel in the middle of a hospital, so I decided against it, although that's exactly what I felt like doing. That beautiful babe was Jack's sister! From the look on his face I could tell that Jack sensed my relief. He smiled as if he knew what was going on inside my head. I'm not very good at masking my emotions. This interaction was the first time we touched on the ticklish subject of what was going on between us. And something was definitely going on. Yes, definitely. *Oh, my goodness.*

He locked me into his eyes, causing my stomach to do flips.

"I think war plays games with people's emotions," Jack said, his face serious. "I'm probably about to embarrass myself, Becca, but I need to tell you something. Over the past few weeks I've found myself drawn to you, really drawn. Anytime you come into view my heart feels like it wants to take off and fly. Something tells me that you feel attracted to me too."

Time for some mature bedside manner, I told myself. Jack had just said something that was a step above flirting. Then I ignored what I just told myself about being mature. My filter-free mouth sometimes goes in a direction of its own choosing. This was one of those times.

"Yes, I've got to admit that I'm attracted to you too, Jack. Sitting next to your bed chatting with you is the high point of my day. There's something about you."

"Correction. There's something about *us*."

His face broke out into a heart-stopping smile when he said that.

Life's too short, entirely too fucking short, as Jack found out a few weeks ago when he was almost killed. I'm 28 years old, not exactly a kid. I'm old enough to know what I'm doing and I'm young enough to know what I want. Him, I want. I want this handsome Marine in my life. I should not be feeling this way, but sometimes reality asserts itself. And the simple reality is that I like this guy—a lot—even though he's my patient. *Oh shit, this isn't supposed to be happening.*

Chapter 2

Today is shaping up to be one of those days that gives meaning to the word stress. I had just received word from base command that there was a troop plane crash about 60 miles away. There were 15 survivors, all suffering from a variety of wounds. Because of the mountainous crash site, aircraft couldn't get near the location, and the injured Marines are being sent here by medical vans. Trouble is, the hospital is at full capacity. It's up to me as the ranking physician to figure out what to do.

As I often do, I went to see Captain Jack. It wasn't just because I enjoy his conversation or looking at his gorgeous face. I've found recently that he is a person I can talk to about anything. I can confide in him and ask for his opinions, and I take his opinions seriously. He is one hell of a smart guy, so who better to talk to?

"Hey, Becca, why the puss? You look stressed out about something. What's up?"

"I just found out that 15 plane crash survivors are being sent here. Problem is, I have no room for them."

"I have an idea, Becca. I've always thought the dining room at the commissary is ridiculously large. Hell, this is a military base, not a luxury dining facility. I recall that there's a moveable wall in the cafeteria that can cut the room in half. How far out are the wounded people?" "About an hour away."

"Plenty of time. I suggest that you close the wall in the dining room and create a makeshift hospital. From my recollection, I'm sure the room will be more than large enough to accommodate 15 new patients. With an hour to prepare, you have plenty of time to disinfect the room and move in beds and equipment."

Oh my God, Jack just nailed the answer to my problem. Have I mentioned that this guy is the real deal?

"Jack, you are amazing! What a fabulous idea. You just saved my day, not to mention the day of those 15 wounded Marines. I'm going to get right on this."

I called the base commander and told him about Jack's idea. Colonel Clarke said he'd need some time to consider it. People tell me that I have a calm, pleasant personality. Maybe. Sometimes. This was not one of those times. I drilled my eyes into Colonel Clarke's and made it clear that I was not prepared to put up with any shit. Clarke knows that I'm not in the Navy as a career, that I'm not a "lifer," and therefore I could scarcely give a rat's ass whatever he wrote in my fitness report. He also knows that I don't care about his bureaucratic desire for delay. He relented and passed the word to base building command that they should follow my demands about converting half the cafeteria into a hospital. I think he was worried that I'd kick him in the nuts. He was right to be worried. In 45 minutes, the wall was closed, the room disinfected, and the beds moved in. I couldn't wait to tell Jack—and to thank him for his brilliant idea. After two hours I had finished supervising the hospital set-up and the care plan for our new patients.

I walked to the main hospital and went straight to Jack's bed. I grabbed his hand. I told him about the makeshift hospital, and that it was all because of him. A few people milled about, and that was the only reason I didn't kiss him.

"Hey, Jack, this morning I realized something. You're not just a patient but a friend, a good friend."

"How about amending that to *boy*friend?"

A few quiet moments passed, not awkward moments, just quiet. I looked around, and seeing no one, I leaned over and kissed those exciting lips.

"On one condition—that you consider me your girlfriend."

Okay, okay, a lot of adolescent nonsense, perhaps, this boyfriend-girlfriend stuff, but what wasn't nonsense was our growing relationship. It was real, and my God, was it growing. This guy was really starting to mean something to me.

Chapter 3

A week later I bumped into Jack's sister, Rachel, in the mess hall. Recognizing her from that embarrassing encounter where she hugged her brother, I introduced myself as Jack's attending physician. She seemed to recognize me immediately. Could it be that Jack told her about me? I took an immediate liking to her and her outgoing, fun personality, and she seemed comfortable with me too. Friendly personalities must run in the Parker family. I felt like I reconnected with an old friend even though we just met. I noticed that she had a strong resemblance to Jack—stunningly good-looking. She told me that she was an executive with the USO, the United Service Organization, and that's why she was at our base in Afghanistan. The mission of the USO, founded in 1941 just before World War II, is to provide support for service members and their families. It's Rachel's job to keep up the morale of troops and help them sort through problems. I admire the work she does because these warriors sure as hell needed emotional help.

Like I didn't?

We had lunch and hit it off like a couple of old girlfriends. I thought it would be inappropriate to ask her about Jack's background, but screw it, sometimes being appropriate is overrated. I already knew a lot about Jack from our endless conversations, but I was dying to hear a sibling's point of view.

"So, tell me a few things about your handsome brother."

"Well, Jack is one of the smartest human beings I've ever met," she said. "Before he joined the Marines, he studied at Columbia University and graduated in the top 10 percent of his class. He can talk about a vast number of topics, everything from military operations, to science, to history. He even wrote a book in his senior year."

She reached into her bag and handed me a copy of *Desert Memories*. I told her I had already read it. She smiled and flashed a knowing wink.

I told her all about Jack's idea of converting part of the base cafeteria into a hospital, saving the day for 15 wounded Marines. She smiled, as if not surprised at all about the story. "That is so typical of Jack," she said. "Show him a problem and he'll give you a solution." She's obviously a big fan of her brother.

"Yup, my brother is one sharp guy. But since I arrived at this camp, I've noticed something different about him, quite different."

"What's that?" I asked.

"There seems to be only one topic he wants to talk about— *you*. I think my brother is in love, Becca."

My heart was pounding so much I almost lost my lunch. I figured it was no time to hold back from my new buddy.

"I'll be honest with you, Rachel. Although it's frowned upon for a doctor to be romantically involved with a patient,

I have to admit that Jack and I seem to have formed a close relationship without even trying. We haven't flat out told each other, but, I'm embarrassed to say, I think we're falling in love."

"Jack's already fallen, Becca. Hey, it's not my job to give romantic advice, but if I were you, I'd go after him without letup. He wants to be your man, and if I were you, I'd make him just that. Hell, every female on this base would like to make him her guy, so don't waste time. You're a beautiful woman and he's a beautiful man. I can't help but notice that there's some high voltage electricity between you two, hon, and I suggest that you throw the switch to the *on* position. Make it happen, my friend. Life's too fucking short, Becca."

I seem to recall saying just that to myself. I had a great time talking to my new pal, Rachel. I fantasized that she may become my sister-in-law some day. Please God, make that happen.

She's absolutely right. It's time to make Jack my man, not just my boyfriend, but *my man*. Definitely time.

Chapter 4

Among the few talents I've picked up in life, foreign language is one of them. Learning to understand and speak a foreign language is as natural to me as breathing. I speak fluent French, German, Italian, and Spanish. Recently our base hospital has been chosen to house wounded enemy soldiers, if you can refer to a terrorist as a soldier. So that I could communicate with them I figured I'd learn Arabic. Within three weeks I was basically fluent in the language, which wasn't easy because Arabic is unlike any of the other tongues I speak. Like I said, foreign languages come naturally to me.

Colonel Harry Clark, the base commander, called me to his office.

"Good morning, Lieutenant Lang," he said, smiling and winking at me. This guy hits on me so often I feel like a punching bag. *Sorry, Colonel, there's a man named Jack, and you're not him.*

"It's come to my attention that you are basically fluent in Arabic. Well, as you know, our base has been chosen to care for wounded enemy soldiers at its hospital. I'm assigning the task of watching over them to you. Do not, under any circumstances, let them know that you speak Arabic. Just listen, don't talk. Your major job from a military point of view, is to gather intelligence. You will listen to what they say and report to me. I hope you don't have a problem with that, Lieutenant."

"Colonel, my primary job as a physician is to care for the people I attend. But I also care for my country. I have no ethical problem whatsoever with spying on those creeps."

"I fully expected you to say that, Rebecca, I mean Lieutenant. You will begin your duties tomorrow."

Although I didn't have a problem with my new assignment, I did have a question, a big one.

"Colonel, I hope that I'll still be able to check up on the troops on whom I've performed surgery." No way in hell would I go through a day without seeing Jack.

"I see no problem with that, Lieutenant. I know that you like to make sure your surgical patients are mending, especially Captain Parker," he said with a wink.

"Oh yeah, he's that guy with the bad shoulder wound," I said, trying in vain to appear indifferent. I was relieved to see that Colonel Clark knows that Jack and I are an item. But I was a bit concerned that we're too obvious about our feelings, and I resolved to keep our relationship to ourselves. I'll only kiss him when I'm sure nobody is around. Jack and I spend a lot of time making sure nobody's around.

Chapter 5

The next day I began my assignment as attending physician for our jihadi guests. On Colonel Clarke's orders, I didn't speak to any of them, but I listened carefully, very carefully. And did I ever get an earful. On my first day watching over the enemy soldiers, I heard two guys talking about a planned bomb insertion plot at the air base. The intent, apparently, was to insert time bombs on our aircraft and blow them up in midflight. I immediately went to Colonel Clarke's office to tell him what I'd heard.

"So nice to see you again, Lieutenant Lang," he said with a flirty smile. *Hey chill, bozo, you aren't Jack.*

"Colonel, I heard two enemy soldiers talking about a bomb insertion plot on the airfield. From what I overheard, they want to place time bombs on our aircraft. I recommend, sir, that we investigate immediately."

"Outstanding work, Lieutenant. You're one hell of a fine officer besides being an excellent doctor. Please continue to keep you ears open. I'll get on this right away."

He may be a pain-in-the-ass flirt, but Colonel Clarke is an excellent military leader. Within two days, 10 enemy soldiers were picked up who were involved with the bomb insertion plot. Their identities were supplied by me and my Arabic ears. They were sent to a special unit, which was run by my friend, Dr. Marlene Patton, Major, United States Army. Marlene is a great granddaughter of General George S. Patton, 'Ole Blood and Guts,' the legendary WWII hero. Like her great grandpa, Dr. Marlene thinks of herself as a tough soldier. She talks and carries herself more like a military officer than a doctor. I almost felt sorry for her new jihadi "patients." Almost.

My spying did the trick. I felt good, proud, actually. I love being a doctor, but it felt great to be part of my country's military mission. Thanks to my spying, 10 jihadi patients are now more prisoners than patients, and they'll be under the "loving care" of Dr. Patton.

I returned to the hospital unit where the jihadi patients were housed. Because I never spoke to them, they didn't know that I understand Arabic. I heard two men talking. The subject of the conversation was me. *Yes, me.*

"Hey, Ali, that Doctor Lang is one gorgeous, sexy bitch. Maybe if you hold her arms, I can plug one up her ass."

I bit my tongue, fantasizing about removing this guy's testicles and shoving them into his filthy mouth. No doubt about it, these jihadi patients were trying my patience.

Chapter 6

I stopped by Jack's bed during my normal rounds, abbreviated because of my new rule as jihadi spy-in-chief. According to regulations, *my* regulations, Jack is required to walk around using a walker in case he gets dizzy. Sitting in one spot or lying down all day is no way to heal from an injury. Using a walker with a shoulder injury can be a bitch, but the idea is to just push the thing with your good arm and be ready to grab hold if you get dizzy. I was happy to see that he was following my regs. Actually, I was just plain happy to see him.

"Hey, Bec, I want to talk to you about something."

For some insane reason, my insides get all tingly when he shortens my name to "Bec." I think it sounds more intimate. Imagine that, getting excited when he calls me by his self-selected nickname? But I've already told you about my warm feelings toward Jack. My feelings are about to take a big shift, a positive shift. Check this out.

"Bec, honey, I've told you many times how impressed I am with your medical brilliance. I mean shit, I thought I'd lose my left arm but now it's on the mend, thanks to you. I've also told you, countless times as I recall, how attracted I am to you.

But this morning I heard something that has positively blown my mind. I heard about that intelligence gathering you did in the jihadi unit that prevented our aircraft from being rigged with bombs. You put your life at risk, and you performed with a hell of a lot of courage. If the jihadis caught on you could have been in serious trouble. They would have taken you out. By that I mean they would have killed you."

"But I thought that information was totally secret."

"Hey, I'm a platoon leader, remember. Part of my ongoing job is to keep my ears open. And my ears told me that you aren't just a talented doctor, you are one hell of a fine military officer. I hereby officially pronounce you *one tough grunt*, despite the fact that you're beautifully feminine. I don't see anything wrong with admiring a person to whom I'm attracted. And I do admire you. And I sure as hell am attracted to you. This morning you went from being my girlfriend to being a fellow comrade in arms. You're the best, baby."

Yes, this morning our relationship shifted. To hear a military hero like Jack refer to me as a "comrade in arms," got to my heart in a new way. If it's at all possible, my feelings for him have gotten even stronger. Hell, he thinks I'm a "tough grunt," serious words of praise from a brave guy like Jack. As I was leaving his bedside to continue my rounds, he grabbed my hand and said something I'll remember forever.

"Hey, Bec, I've been meaning to tell you something."

"What's that, Jack?"

"I love you."

Chapter 7

He loves me! Holy shit, I've really gotten to liking this guy, and he just said the three magic words. All of a sudden I was glad I was assigned to Afghanistan, really glad.

A week later I got another call from Colonel Clarke. He had backed off with his flirting, which made me feel a lot better about dealing with him. He's a handsome, charming guy, but there is only one man who has my heart, a man who loves me, a man I love.

Memo to file: Tell Jack I love him. He said it, and now it's my turn.

"Lieutenant Lang, we have a problem, a big one. There's a virus loose on the base, a bad one. More than 20 people have come down with it and three have died—yes died."

"Why wasn't I notified?"

"I didn't call you because Lieutenant Jackson oversees health problems on the base. I'm changing that immediately and putting you in charge. You did a fabulous job spying on the jihadi soldiers, and now you have a bigger job, an urgent one. I should have researched your background more carefully. My God, you are one of the country's leading experts on infectious diseases. I read that you even published an article in the *New England Journal of Medicine* that has become a standard reference work in the field. Also, you'll be happy to know, I'm promoting you to Lieutenant Commander. Congress just passed a new law enabling a commanding officer to take that step under extraordinary circumstances. And you are one extraordinary officer. You have a big job in front of you, Commander, and I know you will handle it well."

I guess I should have felt flattered by his praise and my promotion, but what I really felt was a need to get into action, fast action. When dealing with an infectious disease, sitting around and doing nothing is not a proper response. Sometimes having a hyper Type-A personality works in your favor.

"Colonel, I have a big question. You just said you're putting me in charge of fighting this virus. My question is, will you listen to me and follow my recommendations explicitly?"

"Commander, although I'm still duty bound to oversee this operation, you have my word that I will follow your recommendations, *explicitly* as you put it. Hell, you're the expert."

"Great. The most important thing at this point is speed. We need to put my recommendations into action fast. First, I insist that every person on this base, yes, every person, including you and me, wear a medical mask at all times, and I want it to be a court-martial offence to refuse to do so. I'll have my assistant check on inventory and order more masks as needed. Also, all personnel should wash their hands with soap and water for 20 seconds any chance they get, especially after coming into contact with another person. I'm also ordering hand disinfectant bottles to be disbursed on stands every 50 feet in every building on the base, and at the entrance and exit doors to every room. Next, I want you to immediately promulgate a rule that all personnel need to keep at least six feet between them and others *at all times*. This is called *Personal Distancing*, known among civilians as *Social Distancing*. I'll give you these rules in writing and I suggest that you tape them to your desk. We can beat this thing, Colonel, but it will take strict adherence to my rules."

After meeting with Colonel Clarke, I met with Lieutenant Dr. Phil Jackson, my predecessor as head of the base health unit. Jackson is a good man, a no bullshit guy who takes his assignments seriously. He wasn't at all upset that I had replaced him, and I was relieved to see that. Nothing like working with a subordinate who holds a grudge against you. He had read about my work on infectious diseases, and he realized that I know what I'm doing. I walked into his office wearing a mask and placed one on his desk. I sat in front of him, six feet away.

We placed a call to the Centers for Disease Control and Prevention (CDC) in Atlanta, which Lt. Jackson had already contacted. I spoke to the director, Dr. Maxwell Morton, a man who I had gotten to know as I wrote my *New England Journal of Medicine* article. I had interviewed him and his colleagues extensively. Dr. Morton and I had become friends since I wrote that article, and he constantly tried to recruit me to work for the CDC.

"I have some great news for you, Becca and I was about to call you," Dr. Morton said. "Colonel Clarke told me that he put you in charge of the operation, thank God. He couldn't have chosen a better officer. So, here's the good news. We've isolated the strain of virus, and I'm happy to say that we have a vaccine. It's a rare virus but thank God we've isolated it. Your insistence on face mask-wearing, hand washing, and personal distancing were brilliant, Becca. Your fast actions nipped the contagion in the bud. I suggest that you keep the rules in place for another couple of weeks. I just emailed you the prescription for the drug. Once again, I request that you consider working for the CDC, Becca. God knows we can use your brilliance here."

Oh my God, we have a vaccine. A vaccine can be used to prevent an infection in the future and can also be used therapeutically on someone already infected.

So, we dodged a bullet, a big bullet. Because the airbase isn't gigantic, with just under a thousand people assigned, we were able to perform regular testing for the virus. Within three weeks we were convinced that we had eliminated the virus from Bagram Airfield.

Yes, I nailed it. Hey, it's my job.

After I declared the contagion over, Jack and I found a quiet and private spot in the corner of the hospital. We kissed, for the first time in weeks. Oh my God, had I missed those lips.

"You're brilliant, Becca, just plain brilliant, my favorite *tough grunt*. Hey, congratulations on your promotion, Commander. You now officially outrank me. Do I need to salute you?"

"Only when you want a kiss, wiseguy. Hey, Jack, commander sounds nice, but I prefer that you call me what you usually do."

"Aye, aye, Sweetheart."

"Jack, I should mention something."

"What's that?"

"I love you."

Chapter 8

Rachel had completed her assignment to Bravo Company and took off for the States the following day, as soon as she cleared virus testing. We promised to get together and were happy to learn that we lived a few miles from each other on Long Island. Yes, Rachel is my new good buddy. Hell, she comes from an excellent family. Quite excellent.

I just found some great news and I'm dying to tell Jack. He's no longer hospitalized so I went to the physical therapy building where Jack was working out to get his shoulder back in shape. He was standing in the corner lifting barbells, wearing shorts and a tee shirt. My God does he have a fabulous build, a flawless muscular body that causes my mind to think dirty thoughts. And I'm a doctor! Although my virus safety rules were no longer in effect, I wished I could formulate a rule to require all women (*except me*) to keep six feet away from Jack.

Nobody else was in the room. When I walked up to him wearing my perma-smile, he reached out and wrapped his long muscular arms around me. By then we were no longer holding back on our feelings about each other, although we tried, sometimes in vain, to keep it private. We hugged, a long tight hug. I never wanted to let go of him. Hey, I'm a diligent physician after all, and that means staying close to my patients. Some more than others. He lowered his head and ran his lips across mine, a gentle, tentative kiss. Thank God we cured that virus, because kissing was definitely not on the list of approved protocols. Then we dropped into a deep, wet, hungry kiss. He may have been hot and sweaty from his workout, but I couldn't breathe in enough of him. He smelled all man—*my* man. Have I mentioned that life's too short?

"I've got fabulous news, honey," I said as we reluctantly let go of each other. Recently we've gotten into calling each other by sweet nothings. I often call him honey, and I love it when he does the same. "DOD has just announced some cutbacks in Afghanistan. I'm scheduled to muster out next month, two weeks before you." Another kiss, this one even deeper. "And I also have some more immediate news. My roommate has just been discharged and she moved out of our hut this afternoon. So, I'm all alone tonight."

"Do you want to be alone?" He asked, staring at me with those sexy eyes.

"Not one bit," I said. "Maybe I should invite a few friends over and have a party," my inner wiseass joked.

"I think the party should consist of only two people. I'm not a doctor, but I think I'll make a house call tonight. I want to make love to you, Becca. I want to feel your body next to mine, with me inside you. I want us to feel like one person."

He's not only sexy, he has a wonderful way with sexy words. A stray thought entered my mind. After our constant words of affection, our fondling, and our kissing, we were missing

something. We'd never made love. That will soon change.

"I want to make love to you too, Jack. You know why?"

"Okay, Why?"

"Because I love you."

Chapter 9

E ver since I was a little girl, I've wanted to be a doctor. I had excellent grades in high school and college, so it looked like it could happen. Big roadblock, however. My parents made excellent money with their big software company, but I hated the idea of taking advantage of them. I love them to pieces, and no way in hell would I become a leech. They were quite emphatic that they'd pay for whatever education I wanted, but I wouldn't hear of it. I insisted I'd take care of it myself.

Although it looked like I'd get accepted into medical school, the idea of paying off hundreds of thousands of dollars in student loans bothered the hell out of me. I read that the *average* medical school debt is over $230,000. What if I wanted to be a general practitioner instead of one of the high paying specialties like dermatology or gastroenterology? How does a modestly paid general practitioner pay off a mountain of debt? So, I did a lot of research, which is something I'm good at, and decided I'd shoot for a HPSP military scholarship (Health Professionals Scholarship Program). It provided for a $20,000 signing bonus, a $2,100 per month stipend, plus the salary of a Navy ensign while in school, rising to the salary of a full lieutenant once I began active duty as a physician. Not big money, but a financially painless way to become a doctor. I was accepted into the program.

So, after my recent promotion, I'm Navy Lieutenant Commander Rebecca Lang serving as a combat surgeon with the Joint Services Hospital in Bagram, Afghanistan. It was a scary assignment, but nowhere near as scary as it was for the people I need to treat.

In my 28 years, I'd never been heavy into the dating scene. I loved to study in college and also in medical school. I'm told that I'm not hard to look at and I've been on my share of dates, but nobody really interested me romantically. Yes, I had my looks, but mainly I had my books.

I think I've done a good job as a military doctor. I'd followed the rules, and soon I'll muster out into civilian life with my medical license in my pocket. Yes, I've followed the rules.

But I broke one rule, one big rule. I'd fallen in love with one of my patients, which is definitely frowned upon, but screw it. I'm drop dead crazy in love with Marine Captain Jack Parker and I can't help it, not that I want to. Just being near him sets my stomach aflutter. And when he kisses me, the earth begins to spin and I struggle to keep from falling over. Jack made it clear that he felt the same about me. The night my roommate moved out and we made love, I discovered that there really is a heaven. Making love with Jack was one of the most exciting experiences of my life, and I want to keep repeating the experience. When he told me he thinks of me as a fellow comrade in arms, a *tough grunt*, that cemented my love for him. I'm sure Jack and I will eventually marry, although he hasn't formally proposed yet, just hinted. I think he's waiting for the right romantic moment. Jack's sweet like that. God knows we've both talked about the subject. When we do marry, I won't be falling in love with any more patients.

With Jack, I'll have all the love I'll ever need. If he doesn't propose, I will. Hey, I'm a doctor and I know what's good for people, and I definitely think I'm good for Jack. He sure as hell is good for me.

Yes, he's the one—absolutely, positively *THE ONE.*

Chapter 10

After I graduated from Columbia University, I enrolled in the Marine Corps OCS (Officer Candidate School). With excellent grades from a great university I could have had my pick of careers, but the Marine Corps called to me. My dad and I always had a great relationship and it seemed like a no-brainer to follow in his footsteps as a Marine officer. In my senior year I wrote a book on the days of life as a Marine officer entitled, *Desert Memories*. It was based on a ton of research, which I'm good at, as well as countless interviews with Dad and some of his fellow veterans. The book did well, and it also helped prepare me for my upcoming service as a Marine officer. Now that I'm a combat veteran, I think I'll rewrite the book and add my personal experiences.

I didn't give much thought to the dangers of combat. Well, of course I gave it thought, but I didn't dwell on it. It's a dangerous profession but I think it's also a noble one, and I was willing to take the risks that came with the job.

A few weeks ago, I was almost killed in a firefight during my duty as a platoon leader. Platoon leaders have short life expectancies, as I discovered the hard way. I took a round to my left shoulder and lost so much blood the doctors didn't think I'd survive. One doctor in particular seemed concerned about me, Navy Lieutenant (now Lt. Commander) Rebecca Lang, better known as Becca. Dear Lord, what a beautiful woman, more like a goddess in a medical smock. She would stop by my bed a few times a day to make sure I was on the mend. Even when she was off duty, she'd stop by to say hello. We talked endlessly about everything. It seemed that we never wanted to be apart from each other. We became friendly, really friendly. After a short time, we did something that doctors and patients are supposed to avoid. We fell in love. There was no possible way for me not to fall in love with her. She was all I could imagine in a woman. She's intoxicatingly beautiful, smart as hell, and has a sweet warmth about her that stole my heart away. Becca told me it was against the rules to become romantically involved with a patient. I was glad she bent the rules. It's like the history of my life has been split into two parts—before meeting Becca and after meeting her. We love each other with an intensity I had only read about in novels. I'm 29 years old but I feel like a smitten teenager. Because I was shot, I got to meet the woman of my life. If it meant being with Becca, I'd take another round.

Chapter 11

I'm scheduled to muster out in two weeks and return home, home to Long Island and soon to be home with Jack, who owns a condo not far away in Brooklyn. Jack is scheduled to return to the States two weeks after me. I felt like I was about to write a new chapter in my life.

Colonel Clarke called me to his office.

"Commander Lang, because of your excellent work as an Arab interpreter, I've requested that the Navy Department extend you tour of duty. Besides your language skills, you are also an expert on infectious diseases and how a virus can spread as an epidemic. You taught us well when you stopped that virus in the camp dead in its tracks. That's always a big concern on a military base. You did a fabulous job handling the problem. Your country needs you right here, Commander."

What the hell is this all about? I mean, shit, how much service do they want out of one officer— an officer who's done her duty and who's time is up?

I called the office of my cousin, Congressman Wayne Johnson, the representative for my district at home on Long Island, who is also a ranking member of the House Armed

Services Committee. I hesitated to go outside the chain of command but screw it. No way did I want Bagram Airfield to be my permanent mailing address. The congressman and I had become friends over the years. I explained my predicament to him, and he sounded both pissed off and sympathetic. "I'll call you back shortly, Becca. Hell, you served your country admirably and put in your time. You're not the only Arabic speaking doctor in the military."

Wayne has a lot of clout with the Navy, especially because of his position on the House Armed Services Committee.

In 45 minutes, Congressman Wayne called me with the good news.

"Pack your things, Becca. You're returning home as scheduled."

I've been home on Long Island for two weeks and my heart is about to burst. Jack is due home today. I've been staying at my parents' house in East Islip, Long Island. The place was huge with eight bedrooms and was situated on 3.2 landscaped acres on the lovely Champlin Creek, which empties into the Great South Bay. I had my own suite to myself. It consisted of a large bedroom, two full bathrooms, and a den with a lovely view of the creek and the bay. Mom and Dad are quite loaded as owners of a large software company that specializes in medical billing. Soon, when I find a position as a doctor, I'll get my own place. But I wasn't in a hurry, and my parents couldn't have been more accommodating. I expect that Jack will soon pop the big question and we'll be looking to find a place for *us*. Meanwhile he can sleep right here with me, although I don't think a lot about the "sleep" part. If he doesn't formally propose, I will. Tonight, Jack will be in my arms. My

God am I in love with that guy.

But I'm a bit upset, more than a bit. The last return text or email I got from Jack was eight hours ago. His words were typically sweet. "I can't really say in writing what I want to say, but I think you know what the words are. I love you, Becca. XXX/OOO. Jack"

Yes, it was a sweet message, typical of Jack, but where the hell is he and why hasn't he texted me back? Could it possibly be that he's flipped his mind and decided that I'm just too soon for him? After all, he is a strikingly handsome single guy and women are attracted to him like iron filings to a magnet. Maybe he figured our brief infatuation was just that, a wartime infatuation. All my life I've struggled with self-doubt, and this was one of those times. I mean, shit, I'm crazy in love with this man, but there's something about a cell phone staring back at you without a message that you've been expecting. He was on a charter military flight and the rules strictly forbade cell phone use in flight. But his flight landed over an hour ago—a friggin hour ago—so where the hell is his text, or his phone call? Yes, I called and texted him, constantly. But no reply.

I called Jack's sister, Rachel. She just finished her term with the USO, and now works out of her house as a freelance editor and part-time real estate broker for high-end properties, a few minutes from my parents' house. In the short time we've known each other, Rachel had become my best friend, my BFF. Rachel and I are always there for each other, and I sure as hell needed her support after so many hours of silence from her brother Jack. I told her all about Jack's short text, and she was going crazy with questions, like me.

Rachel was at the house in ten minutes. Pure energy, that one.

"So, show me the last text he sent you."

I did. She read it out loud.

"I can't really say what I want to say in writing, but I think you know what the words are. I love you, Becca. XXX / OOO. Jack"

"Hey, Becca, snap out of it. This brother of mine is in love with you. I can tell that just by reading his text, as if I didn't know already from the countless times he told me. No way in hell is he ignoring you. Becca, I think Jack may be in some kind of trouble. We know that his plane has definitely landed— over an hour ago—and still no word from him. Why don't you call your private detective uncle and see if he can track him down?"

I called my dad's office. I wanted to bounce the idea of using his detective brother to locate Jack.

"Becca, yes, call your Uncle Bob," Dad said. "He's a fabulous investigator. After you took care of his little girl last week, I doubt if he'll even charge you. You told your mom and me all about your Marine boyfriend from Afghanistan and obviously you're crazy about him. Mom and I would love to meet him. After what you said, I share your concern about the guy's safety. He definitely should have gotten back to you by now. Your Uncle Bob will handle this."

I called Uncle Bob Lang.

"Hi, Becca, I want to thank you for taking care of my little Gina last week. You treated her sprained ankle perfectly and now she walks without a limp. So, what can I do for my favorite doctor?"

I gave him all the information I had on Jack, including both his cell phone and new landline numbers as well as his address. Rachel sat next to me, shredding a napkin.

Two hours later, Uncle Bob called.

"Becca, I've pulled out all stops and I wish I had better news for you. Four witnesses remembered him getting off the plane this morning at JFK. They identified him from the photos you emailed to me. But from there the trail gets cold. Becca, as a long-time detective I'm seldom stumped, but I'm just that—stumped. It's too early to file a missing persons report but I want to let you know I'm totally on top of this case. Don't worry about my fee. From what you and your dad told me about this man, I'm taking this case personally. Hell, this boyfriend of yours is a war hero who served his country with honor, and now he's missing. Becca, I'll find that guy, I promise."

Chapter 12

Five Years Later

In the five years since Jack's disappearance, Rachel and I had become like sisters, although I would prefer that she was my sister-in-law. Yes, five goddam years and not a word from Jack. Whenever I think about him, which I do constantly, it's like a gaping wound that won't heal.

If I told you I'm the same person I was five years ago, I'd be lying. I'm half my former self, if that. In the story so far, I think I've been completely honest with you about my feelings toward Jack. Those feelings haven't changed, but now I'm a fucking zombie.

Rachel and I sat having our weekly lunch at the Oconee Diner in Islip, a couple of miles from my folks' home in East Islip. Yes, I'm still living with my parents, although I'd rather be living with Jack. Thank God their house is enormous, and I have my own entrance and separate apartment, so we never get in each other's way. Whatever shit life throws at me, at least I'm blessed with great parents. Rachel and I have a meal together at least once a week. Rachel had married a nice guy, Dr. Mike Andrews, a surgeon at Good Samaritan Hospital in West Islip. I knew Mike well because I got a job at Good Sam a couple of years ago as an emergency room physician. I'll take credit for introducing them. They live right nearby in West Islip.

Although we would never dare say it to each other, Rachel and I both know the same thing—Jack's dead. Yes, dead. You don't go missing from the world for five years and still remain alive. That thought remains a huge hollow spot in my psyche. I should have gotten used to it by now, but I haven't. I don't think I'll ever get used to it. My Jack is dead. I'll never see him again. A part of me is missing, a big part, actually the biggest part. I love him more than life itself, but now he's gone, gone from my life, but not gone from my heart. At my parents' insistence, I've been seeing a psychotherapist to help me with the issue of losing the man of my life. But sitting for an hour a week shooting the shit with a shrink just wasn't doing it for my head. Unless he can bring Jack back to me, what is the fucking purpose of words? Okay, according to my friendly therapist, I need to get in touch with my feelings, I need to identify what I feel when I think about him. Yada, yada, bullshit. Jack's still missing, and words can't take his place.

So, Rachel and I met for our weekly get-together at The Oconee Diner in Islip. Besides my affection for her as a good friend, getting together with Rachel gives me an emotional connection to Jack. Yes, Jack, the man I love, the man I'll never see again.

The diner has TVs hung at various locations in the dining area so customers can catch up on the news. Rachel and I were chatting when something on the TV grabbed my attention.

"Hey, Rachel, check out that guy on TV. He's being interviewed about that big fire in Brooklyn last night." Rachel turned and looked at the TV. "That handsome guy sure looks familiar," she said. Her pretty face suddenly lit up with pure excitement. Her face matched the feeling in my chest, which was thumping like a jackhammer.

We slid out of the booth and scrambled up to the TV, focusing our entire attention on it. Then we both screamed, yes *screamed*, "Holy shit!"

There in front of us on the TV screen was Jack, *my Jack, our Jack*. There was no mistaking him. That face, that voice, those lips, those eyes. Yes, it's Jack! The announcer didn't mention his name. Dear Lord, my heart was pounding like a drum. I punched *CNN* into Google on my iPhone, and called the station. It took me a few tries because my hands were shaking so much. I was switched to the production department.

"Who was that man who was interviewed about the building fire in Brooklyn?" I said, my breath barely holding its own.

"I'm sorry but we don't disclose the names of interviewees without their express permission."

I almost heaped a string of profanities at the man but opted instead for politeness. Heck, this guy doesn't make up the rules.

"Becca, call that investigator uncle of yours. He'll know how to cut through this bullshit."

I picked up my cell phone, and then handed it to Rachel to make the call because my hands were shaking out of control.

"Bob Lang, may I help you."

Rachel handed the phone to me.

"Uncle Bob, it's Becca."

"Becca, great to hear from you, honey. What can I do for you?"

I explained what had just transpired in the past few minutes, telling him that the *CNN* producer refused to disclose the interviewee's name, but that Rachel and I are certain it's Jack. Absolutely, drop dead, fucking certain, although I didn't put it so bluntly to Uncle Bob.

"Piece of cake, Becca. I'll get back to you in a few minutes."

I'm glad I wore a brown blouse this morning. The color works nicely with the countless coffee spills I got all over it.

In five minutes—wow, Uncle Bob acts fast—he called.

"The interviewee's name is Roger Franklin. He's the superintendent of the building in Brooklyn that burned down. Here's his home address and phone number."

I thanked Uncle Bob profusely. Over the years he kept trying to track down Jack and was ongoingly upset that he couldn't find him. He was beyond happy about our seeing Jack on TV, and asked me a zillion questions to convince himself that I wasn't hallucinating. But he was wondering the same thing as us. Why is Jack known by another name?

"I'm going there now," I said to Rachel. "If he's not home I'll stake out his apartment until he shows up. No way am I leaving this to a phone call."

"I'm going with you, Becca. You can't handle this on your own. Hey, Jack's my good buddy brother and I want to track him down too."

"God bless you, Rachel. I knew you would say that."

Chapter 13

Jack's alive! Dear God, almighty, Jack's alive. On our Uber ride to his apartment in Brooklyn we constantly reloaded the *CNN* interview with "Roger Franklin" which I had memorized on my cell phone. Yes, it's Jack, definitely Jack. *MY JACK.*

Rachel and I reviewed constantly what was going on, not that we had any idea what was going on. The only thing we did know was that Jack's alive. But why does he have a new name, Roger Franklin?

Rachel reached over and squeezed my hand.

"Becca, honey, I want you to come to grips with something. Our Jack, who is now known as Roger Franklin, may have moved on in life. Something in his life may have happened that we're not aware of. He may be married with a family. I mean, shit, it's been five years. I just want you to brace yourself for that possibility."

Rachel's right. A gorgeous man like Jack has women throwing themselves at him. Dare I hope that he's been waiting for me? Could that be possible? He could have simply called me—years ago.

We pulled up to his building, a beautiful brownstone in upscale Brooklyn Heights.

We rang his bell from the entry hallway, the bell with the name Roger Franklin on it. My entire body was shaking—like a leaf, and I was sweating like a beer barrel on a hot summer day. He immediately answered. His voice alone told us that it was Jack. I hadn't heard his voice in five years and my knees felt like they'd collapse. Oh, dear God, I'd just heard Jack's voice, not on TV but in person. Holy shit, it's Jack, *my* Jack!

We had agreed that Rachel would make the introduction over the intercom and get right to the point. I was glad she volunteered because I couldn't put two fucking words together.

"I'm your sister Rachel, and I'm here with your friend Becca Lang."

"Oh my God, come right on up," Jack (Roger?) said. He sounded both excited and confused, but not in the slightest put-offish. He sounded like he really wanted to see us. A good start.

He met us at the door, looking sinfully handsome. A face like his should require a legal permit. He wore a pair of light jeans and a tight golf shirt that highlighted his adorable ripped muscles. My stomach did a twist as I imagined how many beautiful women he'd screwed in the past five years. Or could it have been his wife? I decided to put my racing brain on hold because it seemed intent on heading in bad directions.

"Please come in," he said, graciously waving his hand. I noticed he wasn't wearing a wedding ring.

Wow, what a beautiful condo. It must be at least 2,000 square feet in a classy Brooklyn neighborhood. Obviously,

Jack has been doing okay for himself.

"Since you introduced yourselves from the lobby, you have my complete attention, to say the least. I'm Roger Franklin, but I guess you already know that." He looked at Rachel, and something in his face seemed to register. Then he looked at me, actually stared at me. His face indicated a hint of recall. It's like when you bump into someone in a supermarket whom you haven't seen in a long time, and you know the face, but just can't place it. That's the way he looked at me. I again noticed that he wasn't wearing a wedding ring, nor did he have the telltale indentation on his ring finger.

No way on God's green earth was I in any mood to play guessing games, and I knew Rachel felt the same way. It's taken five friggin years to get to this point. Five years and there's Jack standing right in front of me. Every fiber in my body wanted to wrap my arms around him and smother him in kisses, but, given the weird circumstances, I just stood there biting my lip. I took a deep breath and decided to let my mouth take over.

"You're a man named John Parker, better known as Jack. This lady next to me is Rachel Parker, your sister, as she mentioned. She kept her maiden name after marriage, the same name as yours. We have no idea why you're referred to as Roger Franklin."

"And who are you, if I may ask?" Jack said softly, his voice quivering. I could see drops of perspiration on his forehead. I couldn't tell if he was frightened or excited, but he sure as hell was feeling emotional about something. I know the feeling.

"I'm Rebecca Lang, better known as Becca. I was your attending physician when you were injured in Afghanistan as a captain in the Marine Corps. You were awarded the

Purple Heart and the Distinguished Service Cross for valor. I performed surgery on your wounded shoulder. That was five years ago. I was also your girlfriend, although it's better to describe me as your lover. We intended to get married."

Jack didn't seem to have any idea what I was talking about, although he did rub his left shoulder and stare at me with his beautiful eyes. His expression looked like he was searching for something, searching my face for something. This guy definitely has some kind of amnesia. His gorgeous face went ghostly pale. He picked up the phone and dialed, his hands visibly shaking.

"Mike, please come to my apartment. There are a couple of people I'd like you to meet."

"Who's Mike?" both Rachel and I blurted.

"Mike Smith is my best friend and downstairs neighbor. He's off work today. He's also the man who saved my life, whoever the hell I am."

Chapter 14

When Jack said, "whoever the hell I am," my heart fluttered. Obviously "Roger Franklin" isn't sure of his identity. I think my hunch was right, that Jack may have amnesia. Please God, say that it is. Amnesia would explain a lot. It would explain why he didn't immediately recognize me. I needed to get one thing out of the way. Although he wasn't wearing a wedding ring, I wanted to hear it loud and clear.

"I hope your wife doesn't mind our intruding on your privacy," my blunt mouth asserted. Rachel put her face in her hands.

"I'm not married," he said, "never have been."

Oh, dear Lord, he's not married! Today was shaping up to be a wonderful day. Maybe the best day of my life? My biggest fear had just been laid to rest. He's not married and never has been. As we waited for the doorbell, Jack poured us a pitcher of ice water. I notice his hands were shaking. In three minutes, the bell rang and in walked Mike Smith, a medium height, nice-looking man with an aura of authority about him.

Jack handled the introductions.

"Mike, This pretty lady claims that she's my sister. I must admit that I see a family resemblance. And the lovely woman next to her is Dr. Rebecca Lang, better known a Becca. Becca claims that she was my attending physician in Afghanistan, and also that she was my girlfriend, or more to the point, my lover. I have no idea what they're talking about, but they both look familiar to me, extremely familiar. Ladies, Mike here is a detective with the NYPD, and my best friend. I don't know about you folks, but I could use a fucking drink."

"Roger...' Mike began to say when Rachel and I both corrected him—*Jack*.

"Okay, Jack. I suggest you not have any booze. You're going to need a clear head for what we're about to discuss. Hell, my head is spinning from what I just heard, and I've only had coffee. We'll pop the cork after our meeting."

"Mike, why don't you tell these two ladies what you know about me? You know a lot more about me than I do."

My heart pounded. Roger Franklin doesn't know who he is? That helps explain why Jack doesn't know who he is either. This has *got* to be amnesia.

"First let me call Nancy. She needs to hear this."

He called his wife, who works out of their apartment downstairs as an insurance investigator.

"Nancy, honey, come up to Roger's apartment. Prepare to have your mind blown."

In two minutes, Nancy walked in, a petite, pretty woman with short brown hair. Mike introduced her and told her the stories about Rachel and me. "Nancy used to be with the NYPD, but now she's a private detective investigating insurance claims." Nancy looked like she was about to faint after the brief information Mike had given her. Mike continued where he left off.

"As Roger, or Jack, mentioned, I'm a detective with the NYPD. Five years ago, he was found lying unconscious in the men's room near the arrivals gate at JFK. He had no identification, and he was totally unaware of himself or his surroundings. Medical investigation determined that he suffered a blow to the head with a blunt instrument. Obviously, he had been mugged. He has no permanent brain damage but does suffer from severe amnesia. Although he was totally unaware, he seemed like a really nice guy and I took a liking to him. I felt protective of this poor guy we found unconscious in a men's room. He was a totally lost soul and I decided to take him under my wing. Nancy joined me in the campaign to help this guy. We decided at headquarters to name him Roger Franklin, a name we just plucked out of thin air. From what you ladies are saying, it seems that you know him quite well. Nancy, anything you'd like to add?"

Nancy blew her nose and wiped a tear from her face.

"I helped Mike with our new confused friend. Yes, he had amnesia, a serious case of it. For years I've been trying to find a good woman for this handsome guy, but he wouldn't hear of it. Anytime I brought up the subject he kept mumbling, 'Decca.' We had no idea what he meant, and he couldn't seem able to explain it to us."

"Sounds an awful lot like Becca," Rachel said, as she shredded yet another napkin.

"*Decca? Becca?*" Jack said as he moved his chair closer to me and stared into my eyes. Our faces were six inches apart. A tear rolled down his cheek. A few rolled down mine as well.

"Becca," he said, his voice croaking, "Oh my God, is this you, honey?"

He held my face in both his hands. My stomach was doing back flips. I felt like my entire life focused on that moment. Holy shit, he remembers me! And he called me "honey."

We both stood, facing each other. Totally ignoring formalities, I threw my arms around him as he threw his around me. Not worrying that we may have been embarrassing ourselves, we engaged in a seemingly endless hug and a deep, wet kiss. Oh my God had I missed those lips. After our public demonstration, he sat next to me on the couch and we held hands. I couldn't stop crying, feeling like I just woke up after a five-year nightmare. Jack, *my Jack*, is not only alive, he seems to remember me. He put his face next to my neck and breathed deeply.

"Oh my God, your scent," he said and then leaned in again. "Oh yes, it's coming back to me. I will never forget how wonderful you smell. Like springtime, except sweeter. It's you, isn't it? You're Becca, *MY BECCA*."

He threw his arms around me and we kissed again. I felt like I just got my life back after five years, five *long* years.

"Medical technology tells us that the sense of smell, the olfactory sense, is a key part of memory," Nancy chimed in, wiping tears from her face.

Detective Mike kept respectfully quiet during our emotional reunion. I noticed he sniffled a lot. He may be a tough NYPD detective, but his emotions were obviously getting to him as he watched Jack and me reconnect after five years. Rachel sat there with tears streaming down her face. Nancy was working through a box of tissues.

"Rachel," Jack said, "yes, you're my sister. I remember us playing together as kids. Holy shit, it's all coming back to me." He walked over and hugged her. I recalled that time in Afghanistan when I saw them hug in the hospital, making me crazy jealous, not knowing at the time that she was Jack's sister. I couldn't have been happier to see *this* hug.

"Our chief psychiatrist at the NYPD explained this phenomenon to me," Mike said. "He calls it *traumatic recollection*, when an amnesia victim puts it all together after suddenly confronted by something that brings back his past. Jack's olfactory memory of your scent seems to confirm that idea. You two ladies have brought this great guy back to his life. I feel myself filling up like you folks, God bless you. To bring this all together, let me review a few highlights from Jack's past five years."

He blew his nose.

Jack and I stared into each other's eyes as Mike spoke, holding hands as if we feared to let go. Yes, Jack, *my Jack*. I rested my head against his big shoulder, his good shoulder. I wanted to be close to him. Actually, I couldn't get close enough to him.

"Nancy and I unofficially appointed ourselves as Roger's, sorry Jack's, guardians, although he didn't need a guardian. Except for his amnesia, which definitely seems to be lifting, Jack's intellectual functions were performing at a high level. We soon realized that Jack is one hell of a smart guy. Although he had no resume to show anybody, Nancy managed to convince the insurance company that owned the building that just burned down, to hire Jack as an assistant superintendent. Nancy has a lot of clout with insurance companies. He soon became the boss of the entire rental operation."

Nancy raised her hand.

"Mike, I just got a call this morning from Northeast Insurance. They want me to handle the investigation of the fire. I haven't figured out how to tell Northeast that Roger Franklin is really a man named Jack Parker, so for now he'll still be known as Roger Franklin. I'll be working with him on the case. Something tells me our new friend Becca here will want to help with the investigation."

Mike continued.

"Northeast Insurance seemed delighted with Jack, or Roger as they know him, and constantly thanked Nancy for her recommendation. For the past five years, Nancy and I would get together with Jack often. We had become good friends. He steadfastly refused to double date, even though Nancy had lined up a few women to meet him. He would never say why. But when I look at you two lovebirds, it seems obvious that Jack somehow managed to keep Becca in his heart despite his amnesia. Nancy and I were, and still are, constantly amazed at Jack's encyclopedic knowledge. Sometimes we'd invite Jack over for dinner and we'd be watching an old war movie on TV. Jack could remember every battle before it came on the screen, as well as the name of every actor, even the minor ones. He seemed to know a bit about everything, except for the past few years before we found him unconscious. He didn't even recall his heroic service in the Marines or his getting wounded in Afghanistan, as Becca and Rachel just told us about."

I figured it was time for me to chime in, although I was barely able to talk. "So, I guess you guys are unaware that Jack graduated from Columbia University at the top of his class and even wrote a near best-selling book about the Marine Corps. Jack was wounded in combat and was awarded the Purple Heart and the Distinguished Service Cross for valor.

I was his surgeon. Oh, I just realized, here is Jack's book." For reasons I long ago forgot, I always carry a copy of *Desert Memories* in my pocketbook. I showed it to them, and their jaws dropped when they saw his photo on the back cover. No, he's not Roger Franklin, he's Jack, *my Jack*. Then I handed the book to Jack. Jack's face showed instant recognition, not only at the cover art and title, but at his name on the front cover and his photo on the back. He opened it to the dedication page and handed the book back to me.

"Read the dedication page, honey. It's to my father."

"Dedication: To Thomas Parker, Major, United States Marine Corps and recipient of the Navy and Marine Corps Medal, and his fellow compatriots, dead and alive, who risk their lives to keep our country safe."

Tears running down my face, I said, "That dedication could be to you, honey."

"I hope you folks don't mind, but I'd like to pull Jack's shirt back a bit so I can see how his wound has healed over the past five years." What I really wanted to do was drag him to a bedroom and rip all his clothes off. Okay, time for a deep breath.

I gently pulled his shirt over and inspected his entry and exit wound scars. I couldn't have been more satisfied. I gently prodded, and he showed no indication of pain. I had obviously done a good job patching up this man. *My man.*

"You look terrific, Jack, including those beautiful muscles." I couldn't help but get that in, even though I embarrassed myself.

"I'm sure that's because I had a wonderful surgeon in Afghanistan, although I don't remember it. I do recall getting off the plane at an airbase, but that's about it. Wait—hold on. I can't believe how my memories are starting to flow back to me. Yes, oh my God, yes. I remember being in a hospital and my shoulder hurt. A beautiful woman doctor constantly came to check up on me, the most gorgeous woman I'd ever seen in my life. The only difference, Becca, is that you're even more beautiful now than you were then."

After five long years, Jack is still sweet as sugar.

Jack stood and walked to the kitchen where he grabbed a few boxes of Cracker Jacks from a closet. Some things never change. Jack always loved Cracker Jacks. He'd regularly stock up on them from the commissary when we were in Afghanistan. He took the company's slogan to heart: "The more you eat, the more you want." Besides munching on the tasty tidbits, he got a kick out of discovering the surprise gift in the box. He would wrap the surprises and gift them to the nurses at the hospital. He was like a little kid, an adorable little kid. I used to jokingly call him Cracker Jack.

"I hope the prize is what I'm looking for," he said as he spilled the contents into a bowl. He had five other boxes lined up in case he didn't find the prize he wanted. After sifting through three boxes he yelled.

"Yes, here it is!"

What can he be up to?

He walked back to the den, wearing a smile that made my heart flutter like a flag in the wind. He kneeled down on one knee in front of me and slipped a plastic Cracker Jacks ring on my finger. Oh, dear Lord, can this really be happening?

"I'm doing this in front of my sister and my dear friends, perfect witnesses. Marry me, Becca. I love you and I never want to leave your side again."

I lost it, I totally fucking lost it. Breaking down in sobs, I wrapped my arms around Jack's neck. Yes, my Jack is now back, back in my heart, back in my life. And we're getting married! Everybody's life has at least one peak experience. This was mine.

"The answer is yes, baby. Oh my God, is the answer yes."

By this point, everybody in the room was crying, including Jack and me. Once again, we hugged. I've been five years without his hug, and I can't get enough of it. This was a moment I'll cherish for the rest of my life.

Our wonderful emotional meeting came to an end. I felt like I was in a different world. Sounds like a cliché, but I was floating on air.

"So, when will I see you again, Becca?"

"When? What do you mean *when*? Do you think for a friggin minute that I'll let you out of my sight? It's been five goddam years, Jack. Count 'em—five years. You're coming to stay at my place tonight. We'll figure it out from there. Put together a few things, honey. I want you to meet my parents. After all, you're my fiancé."

Chapter 15

I don't know if you've ever had an experience like this in your life. Imagine someone you love, and now imagine that person disappears from your life for five seemingly endless years. You assume the person is dead. What else can you assume? But suddenly, by one of the serendipitous circumstances of life, your lover comes back to you, just like that. You realize that not only have your circumstances changed, but your entire life has changed. That's what's happened to me. At 33 years of age, I thought I'd seen a lot of what life has to offer, but nothing like this. Yes, my entire life had just changed. Hang in there. My story continues—and gets even better.

After Rachel, Jack, and I got into our Uber, I called my parents with the news. I summarized, as best I could, the most incredible meeting I'd ever experienced, the meeting that forever changed my life. All I had told them that morning was that Rachel and I were going to Brooklyn for a meeting. They were both on speakerphone, and I could tell they were crying. They both knew how much I loved Jack, and felt devastated that he was dead, even though they had never met him. But he's not dead! He's very much alive, this beautiful man sitting next to me holding my hand. My folks were beyond ecstatic. Rachel insisted that she sit in the front seat next to the driver. Jack and I sat next to each other, so close that you couldn't tell where he stopped and I began. We held hands, as usual, our fingers intertwined, as if to make sure neither of us would slip away. Occasionally he would stroke my leg, making me crazy. I wondered if the driver would mind if we stopped at a motel for a while. I couldn't take my eyes off him, not that I wanted to. Every now and then I'd close my eyes and open them, just to make sure I wasn't dreaming.

During the drive, Rachel and I brought Jack up to date on the past five years—Five years of separation that just ended, yes, just ended in the past hour, like a door suddenly slamming shut, *happily* slamming shut.

I insisted that Rachel be at my parents' house for the big introduction. No way would I not have my BFF, Jack's sister, miss the show. As we drove by the Oconee Diner on our way to my folks' house, I asked the driver to pull into the parking lot. I had some serious business to take care of.

I walked up to my old pal, Gus, the owner.

"Gus, I want to buy that TV in the corner. I'll pay you the price of a new one."

"Forget the money, Becca, I was going to replace it in the next few months. My head waitress told me that you saw something on the TV that got you all sorts of excited."

"Yes, I saw my long-lost lover, who suffered from amnesia, being interviewed. I thought he was dead."

"My God, Becca. Is he okay?"

"Yes, more than okay. Thanks to seeing him on your TV, I tracked him down and he remembered me. We're getting married."

Gus wiped a tear from his face.

"What a beautiful story, Becca. Make sure to bring him in so I can meet him."

"You'll be seeing a lot of us, Gus."

"Hey, let's not delay. I'll have one of my waiters bring the TV out to your car now. Consider it an engagement gift."

"God bless you, Gus."

When the waiter brought the TV to the car, I gave him a big tip. I explained what I just did to Rachel and Jack.

"Becca, you are such a hopeless romantic," Rachel said. "I'm going to call the network to see if we can get a copy of Jack being interviewed. History in the making!"

Three minutes later our car pulled up to my parents' house. It was 5:15 p.m. I noticed a panel truck from a local expensive French restaurant. My folks had obviously planned a major celebration, even on short notice. They love to do things big. A huge banner was strung across the entrance. "Becca and Jack – In Love Forever." I was amazed that they arranged for a professionally done banner in such a short time. My folks definitely have it together. I broke down in tears as usual, joined by Rachel and Jack. Yes Jack, my loveable, sentimental fiancé, cried along with us.

When we got to the entrance, Mom burst through the door and hugged me, followed by Dad. Then she hugged Jack. There's nothing shy about my great parents.

"I hope that you will soon pop the big question to my wonderful daughter," she said, in her disarmingly blunt way.

I waved my left hand in front of her with my Cracker Jacks ring on my finger.

"What a beautiful plastic ring," Mom said. "I'm happy to see that you come from money, Jack." We both cracked up. You can't be around Mom's delightful sarcasm for long without laughing.

When we walked in, I was happy to see my grandparents, my aunt Gracie and Uncle Bob, the investigator, and Mike Andrews, Rachel's husband. Mom and Dad don't like to keep their happiness to themselves. Before we left Brooklyn, I had invited Mike and Nancy Smith to join us for the big reunion. As Mike would later tell me, no way could he and Nancy not be there to see their good friend get his life back. Jack was happy as hell that his friends were there.

One of the catering guys carried my favorite TV to my suite. Jack had an overnight bag over his shoulder. We went upstairs to get ourselves situated in our room. Yes, *our* room. I wanted to jump him immediately and do all the things I've been dreaming about for the past five years, but managed somehow to generate some appropriate behavior. Later, I'd trash any semblance of appropriate behavior.

"My God, this place is beautiful. Leave it to my Becca to have classy parents."

I love it when he calls me, "*MY*" Becca.

"Come, check out the view, honey."

We looked out the large picture window in the den overlooking the pool and the sweeping lawn leading to Champlin Creek.

Jack put his arm around me and held me close.

"I really love this house," Jack said. "We should buy something like it, maybe nearby."

"Hey, relax, honey. I make a decent salary as a doctor, but you're temporarily unemployed. I don't think we could swing anything remotely close to this."

"Oh, I didn't tell you about the hobby I picked up in the past few years."

"What hobby?" I asked.

"Day-trading. I may have suffered amnesia, but I still had a pretty solid noggin for numbers and technical stuff. I managed to salt away a bit over $21 million in the past five years. We could buy a place like this for cash."

Oh, dear Lord. My fiancé is gorgeous, sweet—and filthy rich.

I showed Jack the master bedroom and the huge bed we would be sleeping in, although sleep was the last thing on my mind. "I hope this room is soundproof," Jack said. "That bed makes me think about what will happen later."

"I promise not to scream—at least not *too* loud."

───────

We walked down to the huge dining room where my folks had put out a spread fit for royalty. To think that they planned this party in less than an hour. Dad personally walked around the table to pour us wine. It was Chateau Lafite Rothschild, 1921. Dad's not a Budweiser guy.

I glanced at Jack, who looked breathtaking in his starched

light blue shirt, which highlighted his dreamy ocean-blue eyes. I suddenly began to feel horny as a rabbit. I mean, shit, it's been five friggin years. The only sex I engaged in during that time were dreams about Jack. Later, yes, definitely later. I fanned myself to calm down.

After pouring the wine, Dad stood at the head of the table to make a toast. Dad's always been a delightful public speaker.

"Folks, Mildred and I share the joy that so many of us have today. This morning we all believed that Jack Parker was dead, having not been heard from in five years. Today, Becca and Rachel discovered that Jack is very much alive, having suffered amnesia all that time. And now, I'm happy to announce that Becca and Jack are engaged to be married. Mildred and I couldn't be prouder to have a great guy like Jack as a son-in-law—despite a somewhat chintzy engagement ring."

Everybody laughed. Like Mom, Dad has a delightfully wiseass sense of humor.

"Here's to two of the greatest people in the world."

———————

I woke up this morning, as I woke up for the past five years, thinking that the love of my life was dead. I can tell you that, but it's difficult to explain, this thing that's going on in my heart, but I'll give it a shot. I'm not the same person who I was some 14 hours ago when I woke up. No, I'm not that person at all. I'm different. I'm the Becca I was five years ago, in love with a wonderful man who I expected to marry. Try to imagine the feeling I experienced today. To say that it transformed my life sounds like a romantic utterance, but it's true. In the past 14 hours, my entire life has been transformed.

Chapter 16

By 9:30 our wonderful celebration wound down and the last of the guests departed. During dinner, Jack had been sneakily rubbing his hand over my thigh under the table. He would occasionally hike up my skirt so he could stroke my bare skin, driving me directly into outer space. If my girly parts could speak, they'd say, "We're ready when you are." *Oh, yes, I'm ready.*

"We'll be heading up now," I said.

"Dad and I want to thank you for a fabulous occasion," Mom said. As I leaned over to kiss her goodnight, she whispered in my year, "You two have a wonderful time tonight, actually beyond wonderful. You and Jack are meant for each other—forever."

I am blessed with sweethearts for parents.

As we walked into the bedroom, Jack gently grabbed me from the back around my waist. He slowly, tantalizingly undid my blouse and skirt and let them drop to the floor. Then he hugged me. I could feel his excitement building against my butt, real serious excitement.

"I'm going to hit the shower, honey," I said. I hoped

Jack wouldn't make some crack about "conserving water." After so long, I felt it just right if we showered separately, at least tonight, our first night in years. Jack agreed, although somewhat reluctantly. After this amazing emotional day, my sweaty armpits were screaming for attention—and soap. I showered in the master bath, while Jack took his in the smaller bathroom. I hadn't thought about sex in so many years, except for dreams about Jack, and suddenly realized I didn't have any sexy lingerie to wear. I once read somewhere that men get excited about seeing a woman naked under a men's shirt, so I grabbed one of Jack's shirts from his suitcase. I looked at myself in the mirror. I realized that my body was quite fit from my daily run and exercises, and my curves filled out Jack's shirt in all the right places. I unbuttoned the top four buttons to show a hint of my breasts, which, I must admit, still look sexy and inviting at age 33.

Jack wore a towel, which I thought looked completely enticing. I recalled seeing his fit muscular body when I was his doctor in Afghanistan, and nothing has changed. His muscles are still ripped, enchantingly ripped. His generous erection created quite a bulge under the towel.

"You're happy to see me, I notice," I said softly as I reached down and stroked his lovely bulge.

We hugged, a long wonderful hug, accompanied by a mind-blowing kiss. I could feel his stiffness against my stomach, telling me that he wanted a lot more than a hug. He slowly unbuttoned the shirt I was wearing, slipped his hands under the shoulders, and let it drop to the floor. He stepped back and looked at my naked body. "You are impossibly beautiful, Becca, simply astonishing."

I gently grabbed his towel and dropped it, exposing his exciting, gorgeous physique.

'Lie on your back, honey," I said.

I nibbled at his ears, which I remembered he loved, then moved down to his chest. I kept going further down until I got to the happy zone. I kept kissing and licking him. Then I took his beautifully erect love-member in my mouth, slowly working my tongue up and down his stiff shaft. I've dreamed about this for years and it was finally happening. He gently stroked my hair.

"I want to be inside you, baby. I want to feel all of you around me."

He rolled me over onto my back. His long fingers toyed with my love center, driving me totally insane. Then he entered me, bringing me up to the mountain top. I felt myself getting close, and I could tell he was getting there too. Then it happened, a mind-shattering, exploding mutual orgasm from heaven, an orgasm five years in the making. My mind gave new meaning to the phrase *coming* home. I lay there, my face against his muscular chest as we stroked each other's bodies.

"Today is the best day of my life, Jack. It started by finding that you're alive, and now we just made the most wonderful love I could ever imagine. You're back in my life, baby, and I'm back in yours. Oh, dear Lord, I love you."

"And I notice that your plastic ring didn't fall off. I must admit that I'm good at quality control."

"That's because you're pure quality, honey."

I called the hospital to arrange for a replacement doctor telling them I wouldn't be in for the next few days. Jack called Nancy Smith to say they'd meet in a couple of days about the building fire. Jack and I had some catching up to do, and maybe continue to screw ourselves into happy oblivion. Yes, excellent idea.

Chapter 17

Jack and I have been talking nonstop about buying a house near my parents' place in East Islip. But first I wanted Jack to get a feeling for the neighborhood, so we decided to walk to the Oconee Diner where we would have lunch with Rachel. It was only one-and-a-half miles away. I was on a mission—to bring Jack up to date on the past five years. But before we got to the Oconee, I wanted Jack to meet a dear friend of mine, Lynda Moran, Executive Director of the Community Arts Council, or CAC. The Arts Council is run out of a huge beautiful house built in 1842 in Islip, a couple of miles from my folks' house in East Islip. The place was once owned by none other than Fred Astaire. His wife, Phyllis Livingston Potter grew up there. The Astaires bought the place in 1942, at which time they lived in Beverly Hills. It was the height of his career, and they could easily afford a "summer house" on Long Island. People in the neighborhood refer to the place as "The Astaire House." The 6,000 square foot house could easily accommodate various functions of the Arts Council, although the Morans were careful to keep it as a house, not a place of business. The house was situated on an acre of property. Lynda and her husband both felt that the historic house helped accentuate the mission of the Community Arts Council, which was to encourage and foster cultural arts. They would often hold small concerts in the *Ballroom*, a gigantic living room, which housed an antique Steinway piano, which was donated for use by one of the CAC board members. I often closed my eyes and imagined Fred Astaire and Ginger Rogers dancing there. Lynda is known as a tough task master, who knows how to kick ass when necessary. As I discovered when I ran the various medical missions in Afghanistan, making nice is, well, nice, but it seldom gets the job done. Lynda knows how to get the job done. She'd make a good military officer. Lynda is meeting this morning with John White, one of the stellar board members of the Community Arts Council, who is also a friend of mine. John is retired from his work as an educator and is now one of those people that no community can do without. He is a selfless volunteer. Whether it's his church, his choral group, or his work with the Arts Council, John is always there to help. He also does freelance editing for local authors. As he often does, John had his dog Chico with him. Chico is an adorable, medium-sized friendly dog, best described as a mutt with a purebred personality. Chico went from person to person, adding to his growing collection of cuddles and scratches. Lynda and John were expecting Jack and me, although they were extremely busy. Lynda has told me that she long ago learned to put up with distractions, and I guess that includes Jack and me. But we're good friends, so she put up with us.

Typical of Jack, he jumped right into the conversation, asking questions, not just to be polite, but because he really wanted to know what the organization is all about. Lynda asked him all about his background and she seemed quite impressed. "Hey, John," she said, "Maybe we could offer Jack a job here at the CAC. We love to hire veterans."

I jumped in. "Since he left the service, I've taken on the task of vetting civilian opportunities for him. So, let me suggest an offer. Pay Jack $21 million over five years, and he'll get the job done for you." I was joking, of course.

John White, well known for his sense of humor, said. "Hey Lynda, maybe we should offer the job to Captain Jack here, as long as he's willing to be paid with unsecured, unsigned, non-funded IOUs." We all laughed, except for Jack, who wasn't smiling at the joke.

"I have a better idea," Jack said. "How about if I act as an unpaid volunteer and use my day-trading knowledge to help fund the Arts Council." John and Lynda stopped laughing. Although Lynda is strict about not cussing in the office, she and John together pronounced, "Holy shit!" Chico barked, wagged his tail, and jumped onto Jack's lap, slurping his face with doggie kisses.

"We're looking to buy a house near here, so I'd be happy to pitch in and help with the great work you folks do. Becca has told me all about you."

John and Lynda both looked like they were about to faint.

That is so Jack, so typically Jack. He never asks, "What can you do for me?" No, it's always, "What can I do for *you*?" That attitude earned him the Distinguished Service Cross.

Already, Jack wants to invest in and improve the community we hope to move into. To think that he almost bled out in front of me on an operating table in Afghanistan. He's the greatest life I've ever saved. And then I found him after he went missing for five years. That's why I call him *my Jack*.

"Hey, let's not leave this as a casual conversation," Jack said. "I suggest we meet next week and discuss a plan of action. How about Tuesday for lunch."

If there's a hill to be taken, Captain Jack will take it.

After our wonderful meeting with Lynda and John, I couldn't have been prouder of Jack. His investing knowledge is best described as genius level, and now he's going to use it to help my dear friend Lynda and her struggling Community Arts Council. It seems that every time he opens his mouth, Jack gives me yet another reason to love him.

And he's back in my life!

Chapter 18

We left Lynda's house and walked toward Main Street. The street would never be confused with the Champs Elysée, but it was nonetheless a pretty suburban street. We headed to the Oconee Diner, which was only a half mile away, but after my seemingly endless night of sex with Jack, it wasn't easy walking. Rachel would meet us there in 15 minutes. The diner, a few blocks from Lynda Moran's house, is in the hamlet of Islip, right next to the hamlet of East Islip. Some people get confused about hamlets, villages, and towns. The big thing to remember is that a hamlet is an unincorporated entity. Actually, it's not an entity at all. It's really a neighborhood, the boundaries of which are described by a postal zip code. There is no mayor, no council, just a neighborhood. You don't get to vote for people because there is nobody to vote for.

Gus met us at the door, where I introduced Jack. Gus, always the warm-hearted Greek, wrapped Jack in a big bear hug. After Gus led us to our table, he placed a beautiful bouquet of daffodils in the middle. I don't know how Gus knows I love daffodils, but he nailed it. Yes, this place feels like home.

Rachel joined us in a few minutes.

"My God, you two seem absolutely glowing. I guess you had a *pleasant* evening," she said with a sly wink.

"Yeah, we played ping-pong," Jack said, grinning.

"Wiseass. So, what do you guys have planned?"

"I'm glad you ask the question because you're a part-time real estate broker and you specialize in high-end properties. Jack fell in love with my parents' house and would like to buy one like it nearby. It's got to be waterfront."

"Wow, do you have any idea what something like that would cost?"

"I can afford whatever is on the market," Jack said, "and even if it's not on the market I can make an attractive offer."

Because she's Jack's sister, I didn't think we should hide anything from her.

"Jack, why don't you tell Rachel about the hobby you discovered in the past few years."

Jack told her about his day-trading 'hobby," and how he managed to accumulate a not-so-small fortune in the past five years.

"I love that you guys are looking to live near here. I was hoping you wouldn't want to live in the city even though my brother's Brooklyn condo is beautiful. I keep a list of people who are willing to sell but don't want to go publicly on the market. I'll look through my listings and I'll ask around my broker friends. I'll call you this afternoon or tomorrow to let you know what I've found. Hey, your lovely Brooklyn condo should fetch a nice buck. Maybe you'd like to sell it."

"No way!" Jack and I both said. Although we hadn't

discussed it, we both think of Jack's Brooklyn condo as a sacred place, the location where our lives became reunited. Yes, it's *sacred*, just like our relationship.

"I love that my good buddy Becca is about to marry my wonderful brother. By the way, have you picked a wedding day yet?"

"It's high up there on our things-to-do list. You will be the first to know."

The three of us have a wonderful history together, and it will soon continue.

Chapter 19

On Wednesday, Jack and I decided to take a relaxing day off and hang out by the pool at my folk's house. My parents had a big meeting at their office in Hauppauge, about eight miles away. I told Jack a fib and said I needed to run to the store to buy a few supplies. Where I really went was a delightful little lingerie shop in nearby Sayville. I picked out the tiniest red bikini I could find for our planned afternoon in the pool. I also picked out a few sexy lingerie items. After five long years, making Jack horny is my favorite new hobby.

When I got home, we went to the bedroom to change into our swimsuits. I didn't want Jack to see my new bikini until I unveiled it at the pool, so I put it on in the bathroom and wore a short terry robe over it. When we got to the pool, which overlooked the creek, Jack took off his robe. Oh, my goodness, what a gorgeous hunk he is. He dived into the pool and swam over to the edge where I stood. I took off my robe to show him my new bikini, which was so small it barely covered my essentials. The look on his face told me that he wanted to play. And did I ever too. One end of the pool is surrounded by evergreen trees and shrubbery, totally concealing it from view. Jack extended his hand and I took it as I jumped into the water. He wrapped his arms around me, the warmth of his body making up for the sudden chill of the water.

"You know the best thing about your new bikini, honey?"

"What's that?"

"It looks even better off."

He slowly and tantalizingly removed my top and held my breasts against his muscular chest. Then he reached down and pulled off my bottom. We stood in chest high water with our naked bodies against one another. Then he leaned me against the steps and slowly entered me, gradually picking up speed as he drove me into paradise. I reached over and grabbed my bikini top from the side of the pool, placed it in my mouth and bit down. I didn't want to scandalize my neighbors with screams of ecstasy. We both came to a dizzying orgasm at the same time, a glorious watery climax. Yes, Jack and I were catching up for the past five years.

We climbed out of the pool, put our swimsuits back on, and lay down next to each other on the luxurious big outdoor divan, which was partially shaded from the sun by tall trees. A warm breeze gently wafted over us, nature's perfect afterthought to our watery lovemaking.

———————

"No doubt about it, baby, we've got to buy a place like this."

His cell phone rang. "It's Rachel, I'll put her on speaker."

"Oh my God, I've found it," Rachel said, a bit loudly, "one of the best properties on the South Shore of Long Island, and the owners are looking to quietly sell it. I need you guys to see it because words can't do it justice. How about I pick you up in a half-hour so you can check it out?"

Jack and I looked at each other. "Yesss!"

Rachel pulled her Mercedes into the parking area in front of my parents' house. Could the property she found compete with my folks' place? We'll see. The house was just a mile down the road. I didn't recall seeing it before because, well, I had no reason to look at it—until now.

When we pulled up to it, I was happy to see that one side fronted on Champlin Creek and the adjoining side overlooked the Great South Bay. A large sailboat plied the waves in front of us. What an unbelievable view.

The house was gigantic. The tall columns overlooking the circular driveway were stunning, with a hint of Tudor. According to Rachel it was 10,000 square feet and nestled on five acres of beautifully landscaped property. The owners had moved to California, and Rachel had the only key. A lot of high-end real estate sellers prefer to deal exclusively with Rachel because of her brains and attention to detail. We went inside and were stunned by the entrance hallway. Floor to ceiling tinted windows let in a beautiful amount of sunlight, but not too warm because of the tinting. A 30 by 50-foot den next to the gigantic kitchen overlooked the Olympic swimming pool and the bay. The furniture can only be described as classical charm, mainly leather. Rachel said that the place came fully furnished. She then took us from bedroom to bedroom, *10 bedrooms* in all. Three of the bedrooms came with attached bathrooms. The master bath included two hot tubs. Jack gave me a look that said, "I think we've found it."

"What's the asking price?" Jack asked.

"Well, as I warned you, it's not cheap. They're asking $12,000,000."

"Offer them $10 million cash, closing at their convenience."

Jack's demeanor was that of a guy pricing items in a deli. I make a nice income as a doctor, but these numbers were way over my head.

Rachel walked into the hallway and dialed her cell phone. She came back in within three minutes.

"They pushed back with $11 million," she said.

"We'll take it," Jack said, his voice calm as if he just ordered a six pack of Coors Light.

Rachel communicated Jack's offer to the owners and vigorously nodded her head to us, giving us a thumbs-up. We all exchanged a high five. Because the deal would be all cash, which would cut down on complications, we planned to close within a month. Jack gave Rachel his attorney's number and she called him to arrange for the details.

Oh, dear Lord, we'd just made a deal for a waterfront mansion, just a mile from my folks' house. I'm sure this was one of the larger day trades that Jack has ever made. Having Jack as the man of my life isn't only romantic, it's fun. Chasing my gorgeous husband around a 10,000-square-foot mansion definitely sounds like fun. Jack and I decided to give the place a name—*Bayfront*. Maybe not the most imaginative name possible, but it sure did describe the house

Chapter 20

Today Jack plans to meet with Nancy Smith, his friend the insurance investigator, about the fire to the building he once managed. I will ride in with him and do some city shopping, as well as stay at Jack's beautiful condo tonight, the sacred place where our lives came together. Jack said that we should keep it as a city hangout, a *pied a terre*. I love it when he says *we*, not *I*. It shows that we're soon going to be one, but I feel like we're one already. Having a beautiful *pied a terre* in Brooklyn Heights with a view of the East River sounds wonderful, especially because of the beautiful memory the condo reminds us of. He mentioned that he also wants to buy me an expensive engagement ring, but I love the plastic one from the Cracker Jacks box. That day when Jack slipped it on my finger and proposed, he created one of the greatest events of my life. My cheap little ring reminds me of that fabulous moment.

On our way to Brooklyn, we babbled nonstop about the mansion we just made a deal on—*Bayfront*. God knows my parents have money, and I've never wanted for anything, but Jack's big brain seems to manufacture dollars with a few trades a day. He told me that he made $19,000 while I was in the shower this morning. Wow, a 10,000-square-foot mansion on the water.

Nancy said that she'd like me to be in the meeting about the fire. She said that something may involve me. What a building fire could possibly have to do with me I had no idea. We planned to meet at Jack's condo (*our* condo).

At 11 a.m. Nancy showed up. Her normally pretty face looked anything but relaxed. She looked like she was concerned about something.

We sat at the huge counter in the kitchen, sipping the Starbucks I had just bought. Nancy looked at us both.

"I think we may have a problem, a big problem, and Becca may be involved as a soon-to-be member of Jack's family. As you know, there was only one tenant in the building that burned down, the Omega Realty Corporation. Our investigators are certain the fire was arson, a belief backed up by the New York City Fire Marshall."

"So, what's the problem, Nancy?" Jack said. "Further investigation will hopefully show who the arsonists were, or at least point in the right direction."

"Here's the problem, Jack. Our investigators believe the fire was aimed at *you*. Yes, they wanted to kill you. Thank God you weren't in the building at the time. The Omega Corporation was the sole tenant before you came on staff, Jack. From what our insiders tell us, they hated your hands-on management, and when they hate something, people die. They were concerned that you learned too much about the inner workings of Omega. And it gets worse. The Omega Realty Corporation is the dummy name for a company that is owned and run by radical Islamists. Yes, we're talking about terrorists, Jack, and you were in their crosshairs. And now your bride-to-be will become a target as well. Becca told me about her successful spying on jihadis while in Afghanistan. Those people don't negotiate problems, they kill problems. I've been on the phone with the FBI about this. Because the fire is considered a crime, and because of who the suspects are, it's now an FBI case, no longer just an insurance matter. I received a call from none other than Sarah Watson, the Director of the FBI, an old friend of mine. She has a well-earned reputation for getting involved closely with investigations. Sarah wants to put you two into the FBI Witness Protection Program until they can get to the bottom of this. She has one goal, to protect your lives. Becca, I'm afraid you'll need to take a leave of absence from the hospital. Hell, with your background you'll be able to get another position in a heartbeat. I know you guys just bought a beautiful house, but unfortunately you won't be occupying it for a while. I hate to be blunt, but you really don't have much of a choice. Your lives are at stake."

"When will this happen, Nancy?" I said, having a hard time believing what I'd just heard.

"Within an hour. I suggest you pack some clothing. They will provide a personal shopper to fill your needs, so you don't need to bring a lot of stuff. A senior FBI official will be here shortly, and he'll fill you in on the whole process. I'll be going now. Good luck guys, and keep your heads down."

In peace, as in war, life has a way of throwing curve balls.

Chapter 21

A Mr. Rick Bellamy and a couple of other men are here to see you, Jack," the security guy at the front desk said over the intercom. "He said you were expecting him."

"Please show them up, José," Jack said.

Three tall guys appeared at the door. Jack and I recognized the leader, Rick Bellamy, having seen him often on TV. He's the Director of the FBI Counterterrorism Task Force. He's about 6'1," quite good looking, with a studied calmness about him. This guy deals with terrorism and extreme violence for a living, but he had the demeanor of a clerk in a jewelry store. I guess he forces himself to adopt this calm attitude to keep his head screwed on. I recalled that his wife, Ellen Bellamy, is the talented woman who hosts the most popular TV talk show on daytime television, *The Ellen Bellamy Show*. I love the show and watch it regularly, even memorizing it on my DVR so I never miss an episode. She and her producers have a knack for booking interesting guests. I think that Jack would make a fascinating guest, but I doubt that he'll be invited because we're in the Witness Protection Program. I think her husband would veto the idea. The Witness Protection Program was starting to get on my nerves already.

We went to the den where I served coffee and snacks on a tray. I can always spot a coffee drinker a mile away, or so I thought, and Rick definitely looked like a coffee guy. He asked if we had tea. Okay, tea it is. Hey, I'm a medical doctor not a mind reader. His two colleagues sat at the kitchen counter.

"I've heard a lot about you two, which is normal because we at the FBI always research people we deal with. What a story! A wounded war hero is operated on by a beautiful doctor with whom he falls in love. Then, as he returns home after mustering out of the Marines, he's mugged and left with a severe concussion resulting in a mental blackout from amnesia. I'm sure my wife, Ellen would love to book you two on her show, but, because of the necessary secrecy, that won't happen. We'll revisit the issue when you're out of the program. So, let me tell you about the Witness Protection Program. It's voluntary and you are free to refuse, but I don't think you will do that. Getting killed is a lousy way to start your day."

FBI humor? I wasn't laughing, and neither was Jack.

"As you know, we've received credible reports that a radical Islamist group wants to kill Jack, and presumably you too, Becca. They're an extremely dangerous and violent group, a part of an outfit known as *The Committee*. They believe that Jack has key inside information about them that he learned as superintendent of the building that they burned down. And they also have your number, Becca, from the spying you did in Afghanistan. You did a great job and they noticed. You will always have two full-time bodyguards assigned to you. *The Committee* is ruthless when they target a suspect who may have information about them. As you know, Jack, you did provide the government with some critical information about them that you learned by simply keeping your ears open. How your reports got leaked back to the jihadis is something we're investigating quite carefully. I hate to say it, but we think it may have come from an insider at the FBI. The place where you'll be staying is a lovely FBI safe house in the upscale suburb of Cold Spring Harbor on the North Shore of Long Island. I know you guys have a few bucks, and I don't doubt that you'll want to buy the place. Unfortunately, it's not for sale.

"We're good on the housing front," Jack said.

A 10,000-square-foot waterfront mansion? I thought. Yes, "we're good."

"We'll head to the safe house now," Rick said. "My guys here will pack your belongings. You will have a personal shopper assigned to you, so don't worry about bringing a lot of your things. Guards will be assigned to look over your Brooklyn condo while you're gone, as well as your waterfront home on Long Island. As you may have guessed, I didn't have a hard time finding volunteers to watch over your properties. As I'll discuss, you will find that we take good care of people in the Witness Protection Program."

We went downstairs to get into the car that would take us to Cold Spring Harbor. It was a large, black SUV, of course. What do government agencies find so fascinating about big, black SUVs? I guess they think it makes them look badass.

When we pulled into the long driveway of our destination house in Cold Spring Harbor, Jack and I took a breath. It's a beautiful place, no doubt about it. Nothing like our new waterfront mansion on the South Shore, but definitely a nice place. The house was situated on a two-acre plot and was surrounded by a fence. Every 25 feet or so there stood a pole with all sorts of electronics on top. Having served on a military base, I immediately recognized that the grounds were secure and rigged for battle. I thought this stuff was behind me. Jack, the former Marine captain, commented favorably on the security measures. The car pulled around back and we entered through the rear door. We were met by Agent Miles Drake, a tall black guy with an athletic build. He was the FBI agent in charge of the house. After chatting for a couple of minutes, he and Jack realized that they both went through Marine officer basic training at the same time. Although they hadn't met, they recognized each other. They became buddies immediately and called each other captain, often saying stuff like *Semper Fi*, while exchanging a high five. *Once a Marine*, I guess. Miles took us on a complete tour of the facility which was large and luxurious. The American taxpayers take good care of guests in the Witness Protection Program. Although we were in a prison, it looked like a comfortable prison. There were no bars on the windows, but we were told they're all bulletproof. Lovely. I've always dreamed about living in a house with bulletproof windows. Not.

Rick Bellamy called a meeting in the large den. We were introduced to another couple who were in the program, Grace and Bob Maxwell. They were witnesses to a terrorist event in lower Manhattan and would testify at trial in a month. Grace suffered from asthma and was happy that a doctor would be in residence. I never had such a small patient list, but then I'd never been in prison before. I had my medical bag with me, of course. We also had a short list of people who would be allowed to visit, a *very* short list. It included Mike Smith, Jack's friend and NYPD detective, along with his wife, Nancy, who also had top secret security clearance. Jack and I both requested that his sister, Rachel, be added to the list, but it wouldn't fly because she didn't have clearance. That pissed me off because I wouldn't have my regular chats with my BFF. Jack wasn't happy about it either. The three of us couldn't be closer. Rick Bellamy promised that he would see what he could do about getting Rachel security clearance. Her former position as an executive with the USO would help. From what we've heard, Rick swings a lot of clout at the Bureau. At least I'd be with Jack, *my Jack*, and that means everything to me. I was without him for five long years, and now I consider every moment with him a blessing. We were assigned a huge suite with a large bedroom, two full bathrooms, one of which included a hot tub, and a den with a view of the pretty yard. We never made love in a prison before, but the idea sounds exciting.

The place came with a large outdoor dining and entertaining area on the roof, surrounded, of course, by bulletproof glass. A wooden running track surrounded the area.

Jack and I love to keep busy getting things done. Heck, you can't have sex all the time. Well, not *all* the time. Because we're both pretty good writers, we decided we'd write a book based on our experience in the WPP. It would have to be a novel, of course, because of security. Even as a novel, it would be required to go through a strict approval process at the FBI. After that, it will probably be no longer than 10 pages. What the hell, it will be fun writing it.

Chapter 22

Jack and I settled into our new lives—temporary, please God—at our lovely Witness Protection Program residence. We'd prefer to live in our new waterfront mansion in East Islip, but it doesn't look like we have much choice. Staying alive is a nice idea.

We're both fitness freaks and made good use of the exercise room and the running track. For fun, we would run around the track in opposite directions, slapping a high five as we passed each other. Life in the Witness Protection Program makes you do goofy things. We also continued our fitness regimen on the king size bed. Making love with Jack makes my heart pump in ways I never thought possible. He's definitely good for my health, not to mention my libido.

We began to work on our novel. We figured that the security constraints would turn it into more of a pamphlet than a book, so we decided to write a love story. God knows, we have a lot to write about when it comes to love. Much more interesting than a book about the Witness Protection Program. Jack and I have discovered that we have a way of locking onto each other's thoughts. Writing a book together seemed like a natural thing to do—and we'd get to audition the love scenes in real life. Our flirtatious love affair in Afghanistan, followed by finding Jack after five lost years, are like pages of a book that my mind keeps reading. I'll never stop reading it. After talking about the book we did something that authors often do. We put the idea on a shelf.

I spent a good amount of time reading medical journals online to keep up my proficiency. I also contributed some articles. No sense being a doctor if you forget everything you've learned.

Jack contacted his lawyer to form a charitable corporation, the purpose of which was to begin the fundraising effort for my friend's Community Arts Council. Jack seeded the corporation with a $10,000 contribution. In one week of day-trading, Jack had raised $34,000 for the CAC. My friend, Lynda, was ecstatic. John White's dog, Chico, was in residence at Lynda's house that day. When Lynda squealed at the funding message, Chico jumped onto her lap and licked her face. Chico loves to hear good news.

Rick Bellamy asked for my help in listening to phone-recorded Arabic conversations. Knowing that my identity would be secret, I said sure. Although the Bureau has a few Arabic interpreters, Rick said he heard that my fluency is top-notch. I know my shit, I must admit.

I noticed that Jack constantly questioned our FBI bodyguards about working for the Bureau. He peppered Rick Bellamy with constant questions when he came to visit. Jack seemed totally fascinated by the work of the FBI. Jack and I never keep anything from each other, so I decided to ask him to let me into his thoughts.

"Hey, Jack. Even though we have a ton of money thanks to your day-trading, something tells me you're looking for the next thing. You're not a kind of guy who sits around twiddling your thumbs no matter how much money you have. I assume you don't want to be a building superintendent."

"God no. Because of my amnesia, I didn't have much to compare it to, but being a building super was crushingly dull. No way in hell would I want a job like that again, even if I own the building."

"You know I'm not just being flattering, Jack, when I tell you that you're the smartest person I've ever met. To use a cliché, the world is your oyster. I notice you talk to the FBI guys a lot. Thinking of becoming a secret agent man?"

"I've thought about it a lot. My military experience came back to me after my amnesia, and I remember how proud I was of my job."

"Yeah, but you almost got fucking killed, honey. You don't want that again, do you?"

"Working for the FBI is totally different. From what I've read, the only time you fire your gun is usually on the shooting practice range. It's a lot of investigative work, fascinating investigative work. It's a brain job. And because of the expert surgeon who operated on me in Afghanistan I don't have any kind of physical disability that would disqualify me." He cradled my face against his now-healed shoulder. I love when he does that.

"Whatever works for you works for me, baby, as long as you don't disappear again. Hey, to change the subject to something even more exciting, let's try out that hot tub in our master bathroom. I'll even help you get undressed. How about now, *right NOW!*"

Being a prisoner has its moments.

Chapter 23

At 6 a.m. I woke up naked next to Jack, his long arms around me. Going to bed with Jack and waking up next to him are two of my favorite things in life.

"Have I mentioned how much I love you, baby?"

"Not since last night, Becca, but I can never hear you say it too much. I love you too, honey, more than I could ever imagine loving someone."

"Hey, Jack, living together as lovers is exciting, and I'm crazy about my Cracker Jacks engagement ring, but something's missing? Wanna guess?"

"You mean a wedding ring?"

"Exactly. Hey, we have no idea how long we'll be in this friggin Witness Protection Program. God knows we love being with each other, but I really want us to be man and wife. You?"

"You nailed it, baby. Let's do it now. Whenever we get out of the God-forsaken program, we can have a big traditional wedding, which I'm sure your parents would love to host. Or maybe we can have it at our new house on the water."

"I'm sure Rick Bellamy can figure this out for us. I agree, honey, let's get married as soon as possible. I want us to be one, although we're pretty close to being that already."

I never thought that planning a wedding, even a small one, could be so much fun, but with Jack, everything is fun.

Chapter 24

Rick Bellamy stopped by for his weekly visit. We told him about our desire to get married and asked him how we could handle it. Rick didn't look surprised.

First, he had great news for us. Jack's sister Rachel had just been granted top secret clearance and permission to visit us at our safe house, thanks to Rick. Unfortunately, her husband couldn't join us because he doesn't have clearance. This clearance stuff is a pain in the ass, but we're happy that Rick got Rachel approved. I looked forward to my weekly get togethers with my BFF.

"No problem, folks. This isn't the first time a wedding will happen in the Witness Protection Program. Father Rafael Guzman is an Episcopal priest and the chaplain for the New York City FBI office. He's a great guy and has top secret clearance. He's the man to make this happen."

We contacted Father Guzman and planned to have our wedding this Saturday on our rooftop garden, weather permitting. Detective Mike Smith happily agreed to be Jack's best man, and my good buddy Rachel would be my maid of honor, now that she had permission to visit us. I think being a maid of honor at your brother's wedding is totally cool, and

Rachel agrees. Mike's wife, Nancy, who also has top secret clearance, will be a bridesmaid. Our fellow prisoners, Bob and Grace Maxell, will attend of course. Father Guzman's pretty wife, Violetta, who is an FBI field agent, will be there. She happily volunteered to be a bridesmaid. I never considered having a bridesmaid wearing a pistol, but life in the Witness Protection Program requires some flexibility.

Saturday came, the day of our wedding, and I was ecstatic. The weather was perfect, a cloudless sky with a temperature of 74. The rooftop area was beautiful, I thought as I looked at the running track, where Jack and I did our high fives this morning. Jack, a man who I thought I had lost forever, is about to become my husband. I love him more than I ever thought possible, but now on our wedding day, I love him even more.

At Jack's urging I kept my maiden name, Lang, because I had become quite well-known with my writing.

Our personal shopper had gone over a few items with us and got a tuxedo for Jack, and a flowing white wedding dress for me. Jack looked drop dead gorgeous, as usual, but today even more so. Jack and I felt like we were kids about to attend the senior prom. Our shopper, Denise, had showed us a few engagement rings, but I insisted I would continue to wear my Cracker Jacks ring, my proudest possession. She did order us a couple of plain but lovely wedding rings.

While Denise left to run an errand, Jack gently stroked my ass.

"Hey, stop that," I said, playfully swatting his arm.

"No."

"Okay, then don't stop. But use two hands. It's more fun."

The ceremony began at 11 a.m. Father Rafael is a terrific guy. He spoke with a slight accent from his native Bolivia, adding to the charm of the ceremony. Bob and Grace Maxwell, our fellow WPP guests, were in attendance. As a wedding gift, they gave us a beautiful one by two-foot glass etching which Grace herself created, along with a lovely brass frame. It was a replica of our house on the water. I had given her a photo of the house, not knowing the exquisite artistry she'd make of it. I couldn't ask for classier fellow prisoners.

After the ceremony we walked downstairs to the huge den, where Father Rafael entertained us by singing and playing the piano. If it weren't for his religious calling, Father Rafael would make a great night club entertainer. His wife, Violetta, accompanied him on the violin. I find it hard to believe that this pretty, charming woman, is an FBI field agent. I noticed the bulge of her pistol under her blouse. Jack ordered top shelf booze for the occasion, and the liquid flowed. Rick Bellamy and our bodyguards, always the diligent FBI agents, sipped soft drinks.

Rachel, God bless her, raised a glass and proposed a toast. I could tell she was trying to keep her emotions under control.

"Becca is my good buddy, my BFF, my Best Friend Forever. I am so happy I could pass out. Becca has just married my wonderful brother, Jack. If God ever wanted to make a poster of two people perfectly suited for each other, Becca and Jack would be the ideal models. We thought we had lost Jack forever, only to discover that he suffered from amnesia. He never married, nor did he even date, because somewhere inside his confused mind, Becca remained the love of his life. Here's to two wonderful people. May God bless them."

Our little gathering went nuts cheering and crying.

So, the man of my life is now, well, the man of my life. To think that I almost lost him. Hey, snap out of it. Just enjoy the moment, the beautiful moment.

Chapter 25

Jack and I have been in the Witness Protection Program for three months, which seemed like more of an eternity because we had no real choice in the matter. At least we got married, a not so small item on my to-do list. Even though the surroundings were lovely, we still felt like we were in a prison. I filled up my days researching medical journals and writing articles. I worked on an update to my article about epidemics for *The New England Journal of Medicine*. Jack spent a lot of his time studying the FBI. He also paid attention to day-trading, keeping our sizeable portfolio growing. Jack sure knows how to make love—and money. According to Rick Bellamy, only eight men are involved in the plot to kill Jack and me. It was just a matter of finding them, he assured us. Assurances are fine, but why can't he just nail the bastards?

Chapter 26

On Valentine's Day, Jack handed me a beautifully wrapped package. I was dying to see what romantic Jack had bought me for Valentine's Day. He has an active imagination that matches his big brain. My gift was wrapped so nicely, I carefully opened it to preserve the packaging. There, sitting on my lap, was a lovely .38 caliber Glock pistol, charmingly named a Glock 38. There was also a shoulder holster. It even came with extra ammunition! My Valentine's Day firearm.

"Jack, baby, you've gone from hopeless romantic to confusing romantic. What, pray tell, is the friggin gun for?"

"It was Rick Bellamy's idea, hon. Yes, we have a bodyguard, but we can't be too careful. You and I both come with histories of pissing off the jihadi set, and they won't listen to anything except force. Besides, I think you'll look sexy as hell in shoulder holster. Here, let's put it on you."

I slipped into the holster and Jack secured it from behind.

"My God, you look gorgeous with your shoulder holster, baby. Make sure to flip on the gun safety when we have sex."

"Jack, I cannot friggin believe I'm wearing a gun. Hey, I'm

a doctor. I'm supposed to heal people."

"And you do a beautiful job of doing just that. Hey, do you know how to heal the enemy?"

"Okay, how?"

"You kill them—before they kill you. Let's hit the practice range tomorrow. I know you learned to shoot in the Navy, but I want to make sure you're proficient. This is serious shit, honey, deadly serious."

Yes, .38 caliber serious shit.

———

On Thursday, Jack and I got permission to go to the nearby FBI shooting practice range. I had learned to fire a pistol as a naval officer, a job requirement, but frankly never took it too seriously. Jack has convinced me that it's time to get serious. Both of us have targets on our backs and being armed and ready to fire is one way to protect yourself, even if you have a bodyguard, which we do. I was happy to see that after two hours on the range, my target practice can only be described as excellent. As Jack told me, I can shoot the balls off a mosquito at 50 yards.

In addition to coaching from the range officer, Jack helped me with physical maneuvers that could enable me to get off a round on a moment's notice. I learned to duck, twist, and fire; useful talents if you're suddenly caught in a life-threatening situation. I'm a doctor, a healer, but as Jack convinced me, the way to heal somebody who wants to shoot you is to kill him first. This sucks, but I'm learning to live with it, emphasis on the word *live*.

So, pistol packing Dr. Becca Lang is ready to rumble. Yeah, right?

Chapter 27

Jack and I just finished playing a game of Scrabble before lunch. I've always been good at Scrabble, once winning a tournament when I was in college. I've always loved the game and would often play with my parents when I was a kid. Because I'm a terrific speller and fluent in five languages, you would think that I'm a natural Scrabble champ. You would think. But Jack always manages to kick my ass. Damn, he's so friggin smart.

As a reward for his winning the game, I rewrapped a book from our shelf. The title was *Scrabble for Dummies*. I hope Jack lets me read it.

Jack sat at the desk in the den going over a few items with Rick Bellamy on the phone. I had just used the ladies' room. As I walked back into the kitchen, out of the corner of my eye I saw something that didn't look right. The front door to the house was open. Our bodyguard, who always stations himself in the entrance hallway, would never allow this.

I saw a sudden movement. Two men wearing facemasks silently walked out of the alcove next to the door. They both had guns in their hands. They apparently didn't notice me standing on the other side of the refrigerator. They walked swiftly toward Jack, who was on the phone with his back toward them.

"Jack, down!" I screamed at the top of my lungs.

Both men spun and faced me.

Fresh off my pistol training, I crouched down on one knee and fired two rounds each at the intruders' chests as I had been trained. Shoot to kill, then survey the results. Both men lay dead on the floor next to the desk. Thank God, Jack had convinced me to wear my gun at all times, even when playing Scrabble.

I stood, holding my pistol in the air while Jack slowly walked to the open door. He cautiously looked outside the door, and found our bodyguard on the floor, seriously wounded and possibly dead. Obviously, they used a silencer when they shot him. I walked behind Jack, holding my pistol with both hands. We both wanted to be sure we had no more uninvited guests.

Rick Bellamy, who was still on speaker phone, shouted "What the hell is going on?"

"We just had a gunfight with two armed intruders, Rick. Or I should say Becca had a gunfight. She killed them both. Wally Milton, our bodyguard, has been shot and he's unconscious."

"Don't move. A group of agents will be at your door in minutes." Rick was on Long Island that day.

I kneeled next to our wounded bodyguard. He was still alive but barely. I grabbed my medical kit and applied a pressure point tourniquet to his right arm, which was bleeding profusely. Then I debrided the wound and sutured it. An ambulance arrived and the EMTs placed Wally on a stretcher and took him to the hospital. We would later find out that he survived, thank God. I felt good that my immediate first aid managed to save Wally's life. Nice to know that I can heal as well as kill.

Rick, along with four other agents, was at our door in 15 minutes. Rick, our good friend, gave both Jack and me a hug, as the other agents examined the bodies of the intruders.

"So, how does it feel to be a killer of a doctor?" Rick said.

More dumb FBI humor? I wasn't laughing. Everything happened so fast, my emotions hadn't caught up with my thinking. I had never killed anyone before, never even fired my gun except on the practice range. I suppose I should feel bad, but I don't. Those two bastards were out to kill us and I got to them first. I hope they enjoy their time in hell.

"Hey, Rick," I said. "The government could save a lot of money by putting us up at the Holiday Inn. It's just as safe as this place."

Rick didn't have a response, and I almost felt bad for him. This wasn't supposed to happen. Having a bodyguard is all about preventing something like this but it didn't work out that way. Jack and I came within a hair of being killed—at our Witness Protection Program residence. Not a comforting feeling. Without prompting from Jack, I called the shooting range to secure us spots for tomorrow.

Jack walked up to me and wrapped me in his arms.

"That was quite thoughtful of you to save my life, honey," Jack the wiseguy said. "Hey, the smell of gunpowder on you is enticing, but let's take a shower and celebrate being alive. Have I mentioned recently how much I love you?"

On a chilly Thursday morning in April, Rick Bellamy showed up at our WPP "safe house." We had learned to expect Rick on a moment's notice, or actually without a moment's notice. Surprising people is one of Rick's specialties. Fortunately, he never showed up after 5 p.m. so Jack and I still managed to fit in our quiet time together. Rick looked happy, which was a surprise. He always has a calmness about him, but seldom wears a face that could be described as happy.

"Great news, guys, actually fabulous news. We nailed the eight jihadis who were tasked with taking you two out. Five of them are dead, including the two who Becca shot, and the remaining three are in deep custody. So, you guys are free to take up residence at your beautiful new waterfront home. Although you will still have bodyguards, you are no longer in the Witness Protection Program."

Chapter 28

So, we're sprung from the Witness Protection Program, the "secure" safe house where we were almost killed. We're free! Jack ran his hand down my back to check on my shoulder holster. *Once a Marine.* We headed straight for *Bayfront*, our waterfront mansion on the South Shore, with our bodyguards in the car behind us. Yes, we still have bodyguards. As we pulled up to the house, I realized that I'd forgotten how beautiful it is.

As soon as we walked in, we hugged and kissed. Hugging and kissing Jack are two things in life I simply cannot do without, so I never do without them.

Jack decided to stop pussyfooting with his thoughts about becoming an FBI agent. He asked me once again what I thought about the idea. I said that if it works for him, I'd make it work for me. He explained to me many times that being an FBI agent is nowhere near as dangerous as being a Marine officer. The FBI requires brains, and Jack has plenty on that front. He flat out asked Rick Bellamy how that could happen. Rick, who had countless conversations with Jack, was ongoingly amazed at Jack's intelligence. The FBI agent approval process is relentless and thorough, but Jack passed muster without a single objection. He certainly has the educational credentials, not to mention his brave military service. His time in la la land as an amnesia victim had raised some eyebrows, but the investigation of a man named Roger Franklin disclosed no problems. The FBI honchos, including Rick Bellamy, had no concern with Jack working out of our new house on the bay. Because Jack would be assigned to the Counterintelligence Task Force, Rick realized that the FBI needed a Long Island presence. Besides, Jack's huge brain covers a lot more than just miles. And he would work out of *Bayfront*, the most gorgeous office imaginable—five acres on the water. Beats the hell out of a cubicle at the 26 Federal Plaza.

We attended the ceremony where Jack formally became an FBI agent at FBI headquarters in Manhattan in early May. Jack's dad, Tom, and his mother, Jane were there, along with his sister, our good buddy, Rachel. My folks were there as well. Jack's good friends, Mike and Nancy Smith, were also invited. They both told me they thought Jack would be a great agent.

At Jack's urging, Rick Bellamy pulled some strings and got me appointed as a provisional FBI agent. My parents thought that was the coolest thing they ever heard. God bless their positive attitude. I wish I felt as cool about it as they do. But in a way, I love the idea. It will bring me closer to Jack, if that's even possible. After our close encounter with the would-be assassins, I like the idea of carrying a gun. If you threaten my Jack, consider yourself well-done toast with a side of bullet holes. I was scheduled to be sworn in at the same time as Jack.

After Jack took the oath, Rick slipped the FBI Agent badge on Jack's pocket. As we left the room, I whispered to Jack, "So, do I need to salute you now?"

"Only when you want sex."

I snapped a sharp salute. "I'll take that as a direct order, Captain. Later, baby."

We decided to use Jack's induction into the FBI as an excuse to have our first party at our waterfront mansion. All of our friends and family were invited, of course. We made sure to invite Father Rafael Guzman, the priest who joined us in marriage. His pretty wife, Violetta, was with him, armed with her pistol, of course. It was a lovely day in early May with a hint of the approaching summer. The gentle breeze off the Great South Bay made it more than special. Jack, his nimble brain always on overtime, told me that the Great South Bay isn't a bay at all, not even close, because the opening to it is a narrow inlet (the Fire Island Inlet) rather than a wide entrance from a larger body of water, typical of a bay. No, the Great South Bay is really a lagoon, a very large one at 151 square miles. I always thought of a lagoon as a small tropical body of water surrounded by palm trees and dancing girls in grass skirts. As usual, Jack's research made me question my previous thoughts. "Great South Bay sounds better than Great South Lagoon. Just because I call you Becca doesn't mean you're not a doctor." Good point. So, bay it is. Jack is totally okay with calling it that, although lagoon makes for interesting cocktail party chatter. Besides, naming our house *Lagoonfront* would be just plain dumb. Whatever you call the body of water, it's beautiful.

Our party began on the 800-square-foot wooden deck overlooking the bay. The early May weather was unseasonably warm with a temperature of 79 degrees. Rick Bellamy, as Jack's sponsor into the FBI, was the formal host. He brought along his lovely wife Ellen. Because Jack and I are no longer in the Witness Protection Program, Rick okayed the idea of Jack and me being guests on *The Ellen Bellamy Show*, subject, of course, to vetting of questions by the FBI.

At 5 p.m., Rick stood to make a toast.

"I'm proud and happy that Jack Parker, a man whom I've grown to know as a friend, is now serving his country as an FBI Agent, as he once served as a brave Marine officer. Jack's brain probably matches the combined agents of the entire FBI. He's a good man, tested under fire, and the Bureau will be a better agency because he's a part of it. I also salute Lieutenant Commander Becca Lang, USNR, Jack's wife. She served our country with honor, and saved Jack's life on two occasions, once as his attending physician in Afghanistan, and the other time after an assassination attempt. She's talented at healing wounds with stiches as well as inflicting them with bullets. Becca is now a provisional FBI agent. These are two of the best people our country has ever produced."

I had promised myself not to cry during the speeches, but immediately broke my promise. Hearing Rick praise us as *two of the best people our nation has ever produced* got right to my gut. Rick Bellamy has a moving way with words. Jack reached over and wiped a tear from my face.

Dad raised his drink to propose another toast. "Becca and Jack are two of my favorite people in the world. Becca's plastic engagement ring is even starting to grow on me."

I held my left hand to my face, proudly displaying my Cracker Jacks ring.

After the few toasts, Ellen Bellamy pulled me over to chat. I'm no shrinking violet, but I felt like a little kid talking to my favorite TV talk show host. Ellen said that she'd been dying to interview Jack and me on her show, but obviously it couldn't happen while we were in the Witness Protection Program. But now that we're out of the program, she's been given the green light. She reviewed her plans for us to appear on *The Ellen Bellamy Show*.

"As often happens with a few of my guests," Ellen said, "the FBI wants to preview the show before it airs. That's okay by me. I know quite a bit about government security and the need to keep some stuff secret, so they usually have no problems with my questions. But I don't want to talk about that stuff anyway. I will ask you mainly about the wonderful romantic story about you and Jack in Afghanistan, and also how you found him five years after he became lost with amnesia. My God, what a fabulous romantic novel this story would make, but it really happened. I strongly recommend that you and Jack write a book about all this. Being on my show will help make it a best seller. Hey, I understand that you and Jack have a condo in Brooklyn Heights, not far from where Rick and I live in Greenwich Village. We should make it a point to pal around often. Especially because Rick and Jack are now colleagues in the FBI, I feel a serious friendship brewing between the four of us. I'll have my producer call you next week to make a date for your taping. We'll talk soon."

I felt myself freaking out. My TV talk show hero wants to "pal around" with me and Jack. Life has certainly gotten interesting.

A few of our guests were staying over in one of our 10 bedrooms, including Rachel and her husband Mike Andrews, even though they live nearby in West Islip. I was dying for my BFF and her husband to enjoy *Bayfront,* and Rachel agreed. After all, she found us this house.

After the party, Jack and I went to our gigantic bedroom suite on the top floor. This would be our first night there. A full moon bathed the bay in beautiful light, from which we had a great view through the picture window in our bedroom. The suite included two bedrooms, two bathrooms, and a huge den. The two master bathrooms each included a hot tub. Just looking at the place made me feel horny, and I could tell that Jack was feeling in the mood too. We helped each other get undressed and got into the shower together, yes, together. After lathering each other and rinsing off, we grabbed towels to dry each other. Drying off Jack's naked body makes me go nuts for some reason, but who needs a reason? We retired to the king-sized bed with its sweeping view of the moonlit bay. Yes, we picked a great house to live in and make love in. The view of the bay was fabulous, but the view of my sexy naked husband was even better.

Chapter 29

Good afternoon, ladies and gentlemen, and welcome to *The Ellen Bellamy Show*. I'm your host, you guessed it, Ellen Bellamy. My two guests today could have stepped out of a Harlequin romance novel. Their story is one of dedication, courage, and love. Navy Lieutenant Commander Becca Lang, who was a lieutenant at the time, was the physician assigned to the wounded Marine Captain, Jack Parker, at the base hospital at Bagram Airfield in Afghanistan. He had lost so much blood from a bullet wound to his shoulder, the medical staff didn't think he'd survive. Becca's expert surgery saved Jack's life. He not only survived, he fully recovered. If this were a medical story, it would be a happy one, but it didn't stop there. Becca and Jack did something that military people are supposed to avoid, especially in a doctor-patient relationship—They fell in love. We're about to take a station break, but don't even think about changing the channel. Prepare to have your minds blown."

Ellen Bellamy has a way of telling a story that brings the viewers to the edge of their seats. She has a knack for setting you up for the next scene after a station break. Maybe we should co-author the book we've been thinking about with Ellen. She knows how to keep the pages turning.

"Welcome back to *The Ellen Bellamy Show*, my friends. I told you I was about to blow your minds, and I won't disappoint you. After saving Jack's life with her surgery, they prepared to muster out of the service and return home to the States, civilians and lovers looking forward to a long life together. But on the day Jack was due to return, a calamity happened. Jack was mugged and hit over the head with a blunt instrument, leaving him with a severe case of amnesia. So, on the day she looked forward to reuniting with the man of her life, Becca was left alone, and she remained alone for five long years. She had no idea where Jack was, and assumed he was dead. Then, by pure chance, Becca saw Jack interviewed for a segment on a TV news show. She swung into action and arranged to meet her long-lost lover. When they met, the wonderful trauma of seeing his lover before his eyes, Jack's amnesia melted away and he proposed on the spot, giving her a plastic Cracker Jacks engagement ring. As the old saying goes, folks, you can't make this stuff up. I promised I would blow your minds, and I think I've kept my promise. So, now let's talk to the two real-life characters in this amazing love story. Becca, your comments?"

"Thank you for having us on your show, Ellen, my favorite daytime TV show, and I'm not just saying that to be polite. If I can't catch it live, I always record the show to make sure I don't miss an episode. You can bet that I'm recording today's show. I think Jack and I have a unique relationship, and certainly it's unique for me. Yes, it's frowned upon in the military for a doctor and patient to become involved romantically. You need to follow certain protocols, like avoiding public displays of affection. But when I first attended him, something clicked between us, a big click. I realized that I had just found the most important person in my life. I guess I'm embarrassing myself by saying this on TV, but my love for Jack knows no bounds. You discussed that amazing story of how we lost each other when Jack came down with that post-mugging bout of amnesia. It was the scariest and most incredible thing that ever happened to me, or to Jack. I thought I had lost him forever, and a chance look at a TV news show brought our lives back together after five long years. It was an experience I'll never forget."

Ellen, totally out of character, wiped a tear from her cheek.

"Jack, what would you like to add to what Becca just said?"

"Becca and I disagree about very little. Our idea of an argument is whether to use milk or half and half in the coffee."

"Definitely half and half," I said.

Jack faked a look of angry disapproval. I bit my lip and squeezed his hand. Maybe we should do comedy.

"Yes, I totally agree with Becca that we have a unique relationship. Not too many men can brag that his wife saved his life—twice. And it's not just syrupy romantic stuff. We respect each other. She's an incredible doctor and also has an amazing range of other talents. I mean, wow, she speaks and understands five languages fluently and is the nation's foremost expert on infectious diseases. Becca constantly amazes me, and I can't imagine a life without her. I think I'm the luckiest man in the world."

Jack is so relentlessly sweet, I wanted to sit on his lap and hug him. But, hey, we were on national TV.

"Jack, please tell us about your stock trading talent." Ellen said. "According to Becca, you have almost a sixth sense about the risky practice of day-trading."

"I have a firm rule for myself never to discuss it publicly because the risks I take are mine and I don't want people to rely on my words to invest their money. So, I'll only talk about it in generalities."

"I understand that you've made a not-so-small fortune in the past five years, Jack. According to an article in *The New York Times*, you folks just bought an $11 million dollar waterfront mansion and paid cash. Can you just give us a little insight into your investor's brain? What if I say, for example, IBM?"

"It currently trades at $120, with a P/E ratio of 11.86. It's one-year high was $158.75, and it's low was $90.56."

"Oh my God, you just said that without referring to a note. All that stuff is in your head?"

"Yes, it's all indelibly printed on my brain every time I look at the stock quotes. My conversation can be quite boring at times."
"Well, there's nothing boring about the successful trades you make."

"And it's not only about the numbers, although they're critical. There's something about the relationship of my brain with numbers that I can't explain, so I won't even try. All I can say is that it's a handy talent, quite handy. And it pays well."

"And you're a newly sworn-in FBI agent, sponsored by none other than my husband, Rick. I think the Bureau is lucky to have a guy with your brains on its side."

"I'm happy to have Rick as a colleague."

"So, there you have it, ladies and gentlemen, two of the most fascinating people in the country. Because we live near each other, Rick and I look forward to getting together with these folks often. Thanks for joining us today, ladies and gentlemen. Ellen Bellamy signing off for *The Ellen Bellamy Show*."

Jack and I had a blast being on Ellen's show. There's

something about sharing our lives with a national audience that makes me feel even closer to Jack. Letting thousands of people know how much I love Jack made me feel great. He told me the same thing. We constantly tell each other how much we're in love, but national TV made it even more special.

Chapter 30

Over a couple of glasses of wine on our terrace, Jack and I talked about something we had been putting off—writing a book about our lives together.

"There's one thing I've always noticed about books, honey," Jack said.

"What's that?"

"Books don't write themselves. I think it's time we stopped talking about it and just do it. Hell, we both know how to write, and I can't think of a more exciting subject than our lives together."

Among the many traits Jack and I share, getting things done is one of them. Jack's exactly right—it's time to write the book and stop talking about writing the book. We both have some contacts in publishing, me with my article in *The New England Journal of Medicine*, and Jack with his novel, *Desert Memories*. We had kicked around the idea of asking Ellen Bellamy to co-author the book with us, but because we realized that our story is intensely personal, we decided that we'd be the only authors. I did call Ellen to bounce the idea off her and ask about her contacts among publishers. She called her friend,

Tom Bixby, a senior editor at Random House, no less. She told him about our story and sent him a clip of our appearance on her show. The guy loved the idea and called us the next day. And we don't even have an agent! Normally big publishers want to deal with an agent, not directly with authors. Ellen's introduction helped a lot, to say the least. He asked if we had a title in mind, which we definitely did. *The Love We Almost Lost* says it all and covers just what the book will be about. Yes, we almost did lose each other. Bixby, not a guy to mask his enthusiasm, freaked out over the title. Publishers always retain the right to assign a title, but Bixby loved the one we came up with. He blew us away when he offered us an advance of $750,000. I could see Jack's day-trading brain transforming that money into multi millions in a few months.

Jack and I dove into the book with an enthusiasm that we didn't need to generate. The enthusiasm for the subject of the book is part of our lives. The book will be about how our love began, with my surgery on his shoulder and constant bedside visits, to our joking, then to our flirting, and finally to our falling totally in love with each other. Then, of course was the matter of our separation for five years. We realized that the book was almost written before we even put a word on a page.

We decided that the book would be in three parts. *Afghanistan* would be Part One, followed by *Five Years Later*, followed by *The Present*. We would share the writing, with alternating chapters written in the first person by each of us. We figured that way the reader would look into each of our souls and see how our feelings grew. The book would be chronological, showing how our story evolved.

Tom Bixby assigned us an editor to work with, Monica

Lake. After two meetings with her and going through a couple of draft reviews, Jack and I couldn't be happier to have her as our editor. Like us, Monica is a hopeless romantic, and fell in love with our story from the beginning. She agreed with our idea of us authoring alternating chapters, as well as the three-part design of the book.

When she reviewed Part Two, *Five Years Later*, Monica couldn't stop crying. "Oh my God, two lovers who thought they'd never see each other again. A love story from heaven!"

We spent the next three months writing and responding to Monica's excellent editorial comments. Finally, it was done, well almost. Jack and I experienced the angst that most writers feel when they get to the words, *THE END*. Is the book *really* completed? But there comes a time, as Monica patiently explained to us, when it's time to go from writing and editing to publishing.

So, we called it a wrap, and turned the book over to the talented folks at Random House.

The book was scheduled to be published in two months.

Chapter 31

J ack, *my Jack*, the sweetest man I've ever known, convinced
me that we should donate half the profits from our book
to charities. Of course, we didn't know how much the
book would earn, but we figured it would be substantial.
We decided to split it between The Soldiers and Sailors Relief
Fund and the USO. Jack's sister Rachel, my BFF, was ecstatic
over our planned donation to the USO, her former employer.

Our book, *The Love We Almost Lost*, was published on a chilly
early November day. Monica was thrilled over the timing. A
love story just in time for the holidays!

The third day after the book was published, we were
stunned. It hit *The New York Times* nonfiction bestseller list
at number four. The following week it hit number one. Yes,
friggin number one! A short book-plug appearance on *The
Ellen Bellamy Show*, helped, as Ellen promised it would.

Jack wrapped his arms around me. "Hey, baby, it looks like
you and I are pretty good writers."

"I don't want to take away from our accomplishment,
honey, but I have an observation that has nothing to do with
our writing talent. *The Love We Almost Lost* is a true story about

you and me. It's a love story for the ages, *our* love story."

"Becca, you have a way of saying things that is perfect. 'A love story for the ages.' That's us, baby. Yes, that's us."

Chapter 32

To help us manage our huge new waterfront home, Jack and I hired a delightful young couple, Seth and Sandy Lighthouse. They're both in their early 20s. Seth is best described as a handyman, although he has one terrific education. He graduated near the top of his class at Princeton, where he majored in English with a minor in music. He's a fabulous pianist and often entertains us with a classical medley on the Steinway in the den. He's also a scholar on a wide range of subjects. But he loves doing handyman work. He says it frees his mind to write music and scholarly articles. Go figure. Once, after mowing the lawn, he sprinted into the den and sat at he piano. He wrote a song that was purchased by a big music publisher for $150,000. The modest money we pay him affords other opportunities because he has lots of free time. When not composing music, he takes diligent care of the grounds and the technical details of the house. Sandy is an IT expert, one of the sharpest computer whizzes I ever met. Their pay includes a large private suite overlooking the bay, and they have plenty of time to pursue other things, including stuff that make them money. They love living and working at our house. Sandy is especially helpful with my research chores and with Jack's.

Sandy keeps a signed copy of our book, *The Love We Almost Lost*, prominently displayed on an easel in their den. She told us she read it five times and is annoyed that she can only leave one five-star review on Amazon. Seth read it too and loved it. Sandy brought tears to my eyes when she told me that our book is the primary guiding influence on their marriage.

They're both polite and discreet and would always touch base with us before using the pool. Sandy is also a budding novelist, and her work with us leaves her plenty of time to write, and that's what a writer needs—time. Although we have two assigned bodyguards, it's comforting to know that Seth and Sandy are two extra sets of eyeballs to watch over our beautiful new digs.

Jack and I sat on the deck having coffee and bagels with Sandy. Seth was working on finishing one of the guest bedrooms, the only on that hadn't been completed before we bought the place. I think of Seth as the handyman from heaven—and he plays a mean Gershwin.

"So how is your new book coming along, Sandy?" I said. "As I told you, Jack and I are happy to act as informal editors."

"Well, I've got to admit that I've found an exciting subject to write about, if somewhat scary. My novel is about the hordes of jihadi terrorists who seem to have taken on as a new chore the shutting down of our economy, not to mention the destruction of our country."

Jack looked stunned.

"Sandy," Jack said, "I assume what you're saying comes from that talented imagination of yours."

"I only wish," Sandy said. "But no, a lot of my material is based on facts, most of it, actually. My dad is a political science professor at Stony Brook University. He's pretty much recognized as one of the country's leading authorities on international terrorism. He knows stuff that I bet even you FBI guys don't know about. From my chats with Dad, my gut tells me that something big may be on the horizon, *very big*."

"Is the FBI aware of your dad, Sandy?"

"Yes, Agent Rick Bellamy, head of the Counterterrorism Task Force, communicates with him often. My dad's name is Dr. Randolph (Randy) Jones. Because I know that you're involved in counterterrorism, I assume you know Rick Bellamy. I suggest you give him a call and ask him about my dad."

"I'm surprised that Rick never mentioned him."

"I'm sure what I'm about to say doesn't apply to you, Jack, but a lot of FBI honchos are full of shit and like to keep secrets to themselves. I think it gives them a feeling of power if they know something that you don't. Give Rick a call, and smack him in the head while you're at it."

"Agent Jack Parker here, may I please speak to Rick Bellamy."

"Hi Jack, Rick Bellamy here. What can I do for you?"

"Rick, I understand that the Bureau is in communication with a Professor Randolph Jones of Stony Brook University. His daughter works for me and told me about his expertise in international terrorism. I want to talk to him about helping me with our ongoing investigation of terror threats. I'm wondering why I haven't been told about this guy. I understand that he's quite the expert. His daughter, who writes about terrorism, thinks something big may be coming down and she suggested I call him. I wanted to touch base with you first."

"Jack, I was going to tell you all about Dr. Jones, whom we know as Randy, at our meeting next week. I didn't tell you about him before because there was nothing to talk about."

"Hey, Rick, as an FBI agent I don't think I should be in the dark about somebody as important as him."

"Your concern is duly noted, Jack, and I apologize for not telling you about him sooner. I suggest you call him in five minutes. I'll call him first to give him a heads up that you will be phoning. He's a really nice guy and is totally open with information, of which he has one hell of a lot. He's a brilliant scholar and a straight shooter. He's also a patriot who loves his country. Let me know how your conversation goes. Like you, I'm wondering about what his daughter said about something big coming down."

"Randy Jones, how may I help you?"

I liked how he answered the phone as "Randy." No professorial bullshit, thank goodness.

"FBI Agent Jack Porter here, Randy. I believe Rick Bellamy told you I would call. Please call me Jack."

"Great to hear from you, Jack. My daughter, Sandy, loves working for you and your wife. My God, your place sounds beautiful. If you wish to invite me over for drinks, I won't object, hint, hint."

"Hey, it's 4:45, about time to pop the cork. Why don't you come over now? I'm about a half hour away from you."

I almost suggested that he bring his wife, but then remembered that Sandy told us that her mom had passed away two years ago.

Before I contacted Randy, Becca and I had already invited our neighbor from around the corner, Molly Pearson, over for drinks. Molly is a history professor at St. Joseph's College in nearby Brentwood and she and Becca hit it off. Molly is a widow and lives alone. She's a petite, extremely pretty brunette, maybe 5'3," in her mid-40s and comes equipped with a great sense of humor. Becca, my hopelessly romantic wife, thinks that Molly and Randy may hit it off. She's dying to play matchmaker. I keep telling her that her middle name should be *Yenta*, the matchmaker from *Fiddler on the Roof*.

"Hey, Sandy, your dad is coming over for drinks. Why don't you and Seth join us. I'm afraid that we'll be talking about some to top secret stuff, so your part of the meeting will be short."

"I totally understand, Jack, but I'm embarrassed to say that I'm probably way ahead of you. Dad and I talk constantly about stuff that you FBI guys consider top secret."

"That brings up a subject that I've been meaning talk to you about, Sandy. I've discussed this with Becca. Would you be interested in becoming a provisional FBI agent? Your knowledge is amazing and the FBI could use your talents. You will be given a top-secret security clearance, enabling us to discuss deep topics along with your dad. Maybe Seth would be interested as well."

"Yes, I'd definitely be interested. I know a lot more about this stuff than the average FBI guy, so I don't see why it shouldn't become official. Actually, Seth should be easy to qualify. He once held a top-secret clearance when he was a naval intelligence officer. I'd love to include his big brain in our conversations. And he can do his handyman chores while we talk."

"I'll talk to Rick Bellamy about this, Sandy."

"Rick has brought up the topic with me, Jack. I think he'd jump at the chance to deputize me and Seth."

An Uber pulled up to the front of the house.

"I notice your dad doesn't drive his own car."

"Dad doesn't like to drink and drive. Actually, he doesn't like to drive, but he sure enjoys a drink. Uber could be his middle name."

When he walked up to the deck, I introduced Randy to our neighbor, Molly. Holy shit, maybe Becca is right about these two hitting it off. When they shook hands I could swear I saw sparks fly. With her short height, she's one of the few women who actually looks up at 5'6" handsome Randy. It was clear that they were happy to see each other.

Becca walked out to the deck carrying a tray of snacks and empty glasses.

"Let me handle that stuff, Becca. Hey, you're the boss."

Definitely a sweet kid, this Sandy.

Randy was an immediately likeable guy. He's handsome, slim, modest in height, and is a bundle of energy. He couldn't seem able to take his eyes off our sexy neighbor, Molly.

"I can't get over this beautiful house of yours." He said as he looked at the bay. "My daughter and son-in-law sure know how to pick classy bosses. I wouldn't worry about security clearances with Sandy and Seth, Jack. We talk about this stuff all the time. It's like Sandy has a viewfinder and looks right into my brain. Becca, it's a pleasure to meet you. God knows I've heard a lot about you, a medical doctor and provisional FBI agent no less. Rick Bellamy is a big fan of yours, and I must admit, so am I. At Sandy's urging I read *The Love We Almost Lost*, that fabulous book you two wrote. My God, a timeless love story that competes with *Romeo and Juliet*."

He's a complete gentleman, as we'd been told.

Molly Pearson chimed in. "I read the book too, and I think it's the sweetest romance I've ever read. Her eyes lingered on Randy as she said the word romance. Wow, is it something about the view of the bay? Randy is quite a good-looking guy, as Molly obviously noticed, and Molly is definitely a sexy, lovely woman.

Seth put out bottles of scotch and assorted booze, along with a bucket of wines and beer. Sandy had told me her dad is a big scotch fan.

"So, tell us, Randy, what mayhem is occupying your big brain."

"It's not just occupying my brain, it's keeping me up at night. I'm sure you've all heard about a thing called a *terror spectacular*."

"You mean like 9/11?" Becca said.

"Yes, that's the perfect example, but it gets worse than that, a lot worse. I've been studying and writing about terrorism for longer than I can remember. My major book, *The Ways of Terror*, is considered by many to be the seminal work on the subject, I'm embarrassed to admit."

"Don't be embarrassed, Randy," Becca said. "Your book has earned the accolades it's received. I researched the book when Sandy told us about you. Jack says that his FBI counterterrorism duties makes him want to read all of your work. As they say on TV, *You da man*."

"I'm flattered to hear that from one of our nation's great scholars. Your paper on epidemics and pandemics in *The New England Journal of Medicine* has become the standard reference work on the subject. But if there's one thing uglier than a spreading deadly disease, it's spreading terrorism."

"Randy, you mentioned a *terror spectacular*," Molly said. "Please elaborate. You sure seem to be quite the expert on this subject." I was happy to see Molly dive right into the conversation and found it interesting that she never took her eyes off Randy. I glanced at Becca. From the look on her face, I could tell she was already picking out china for these two.

"Becca referred to the horrors of 9/11 as the prime example of a terror spectacular. Yes, that is the event we all think about, but my research tells me that 9/11 could be a fender bender compared to what we may be faced with. I'm convinced that we may be looking at a series of events that will add up to Armageddon, not to exaggerate."

"Dad, I've read all of your works, and I've written a lot about it myself, but could you review for us just what terrorism is all about, its nuts and bolts?"

"Sure, honey, but it's difficult to wrap your head around the essentials, even for me. The common thinking about terrorism is that it's violence with one aim in mind—to change the lives and thinking of the people being terrorized.

That thinking is accurate, but it's going through a radical sea change. Yes, terrorists want to change people's behavior, but it's morphed into something worse, far worse. There's a new form of terrorism we're seeing and will see a lot more of— simple wanton killing and violence, often with no objective whatsoever in mind other than the violence itself. That insane group that calls itself *Antifa* is a perfect example of the new form of terrorism on the home-grown front. *Antifa* stands for anti-fascist, but their actions are purely fascist. Mindless violence is the new form of terror."

"Holy shit, if you'll pardon my Arabic," Becca said. "If we can't figure out an objective, how can we predict what may occur?"

"You nailed the big question, Becca. How do we predict what may happen in the future if we don't have anything pointing us that way?"

"Randy, quite often you mention your research," I said. "Care to comment on that?"

"Sure. When I say research, I include dozens of trusted insiders all across the land of the sand. They fill me in on information you'll never see in a newspaper."

"Randy, do you have any handle on what this event, or events, may look like?" Becca asked.

"From what I can glean, I predict it will be a combination of bombs. Now take a deep breath. The bombs will include low yield nuclear weapons including suitcase nukes. And I predict this will all take place in about three months from now. We may be looking at a new world, a frightening new world."

Chapter 33

Jack and my heads are still spinning after our meeting with Professor Randy Jones yesterday. The guy didn't appear to be exaggerating in the least when he predicted the upcoming terror spectacular. He's incredibly bright, an obvious scholar, and is easy to talk to. What he told us yesterday blew our minds. And he sure made quite an impression on our pretty neighbor, Professor Molly.

As a result of our meeting with Randy, I've come to a conclusion. I need to quit my day job as a doctor and concentrate on working with Jack as a provisional FBI agent. I can still offer to help at the hospital as a standby, but I feel obligated to use my brain to keep our country from being destroyed. And what better way to do that than to work with my brilliant husband. Jack and I are pretty smart people, but when we combine our brains, *watch out*.

"Jack, honey, I've concluded that you and I need to work together more."

"Sounds great, Bec. Can I ask you why?"

"I want to keep a closer eye on you and all those gorgeous women who constantly stare at you and try to engage you in conversation."

What a stupid dumb-ass thing to say. Sometimes when I shoot for humor, I get the opposite effect, like shooting myself in the foot. Jack's face was a combination of shock and anger. Can I blame him? My stupid ass joke went right to the very heart of our wonderful relationship—trust.

"Jack, honey, all I can say is I'm sorry. I'm sorry for my asinine joke. Will you accept my apology?"

"Of course, I'll accept your apology. I love you, including your wiseass mouth. Now please explain about your wanting us to work together more—without any stupid wisecracks."

"Jack, after we met with Professor Randy yesterday, my mind has been spinning out of control, as I know yours has too. I want to resign my position as a doctor at the hospital and concentrate my efforts as a provisional FBI agent. I want to concentrate on saving our country, and I know you're thinking the same thing. Ever since we met, baby, I think we both realize that we work amazingly well together. We're like Rogers and Hammerstein, Lennon and McCartney, Abbott and Costello..."

"Abbott and Costello!?"

"Okay, okay, another dumb joke. But you get the point, honey. We don't just work well together, we complement each other. When we wrote our book together that became crystal clear. Our brains often meld into one. Jack, our country is faced with Armageddon, as Randy Jones put it. Working with you as a fellow FBI agent is a no-brainer. And I'm fluent in Arabic."

"Okay, you've convinced me honey. Just please no more cracks about me chasing after women. There's only one woman who I want to chase and she's sitting in front of me."

"Again, honey, I apologize for my stupid joke."

"Becca, we both know the same thing—we need to move fast. Randy spoke about nuclear weapons. It doesn't take much time to destroy a country with nukes. We need to meet again with Randy, not to mention Rick Bellamy, but the two of us work perfectly together so I think we should start with just you and me. If needed, I can round up some foxy babes to help us."

"Touché, wiseass. Gimme a kiss."

Chapter 34

Hey, Jack, remember that luncheonette in Oceanside where jihadis like to hang out? Rick Bellamy told us about it. I recall that the name of the place is *Ali Island*. Maybe we should have lunch there. I can put my Arab ears on and see if we learn anything."

"Perfect idea, honey. Our most important job is to gather intelligence. We're scheduled to hit the shooting range tomorrow morning at the Suffolk County Police Department range in Yaphank. We'll head to Oceanside for lunch after that. *Alahu Akbar*, baby."

"That's not even funny, wiseguy. Leave the Arabic to me."

———※———

Jack and I spent two hours at the shooting range of the SCPD in Yaphank. I no longer hesitate to hit the practice range. My accurate shooting enabled me to save Jack's life, and that alone inspires me to strap on my gun. If anybody threatens Jack, my safety is off, and my aim is perfect.

Forty-five minutes later we arrived at *Ali Island*, a nondescript place on a side street. We wore casual clothes, both of us dressed in blue jeans. How do you try to appear like a couple of infidels trying not to look like infidels? We'll just sit down and see where it goes.

"Hey, Bec, what do those words mean on that small sign in the front window?"

"It says 'Death to the heathen infidels.' Looks like we chose the right place."

"I feel at home already."

The host escorted us to a table in a corner, but I had the feeling he would like to escort us out the back door. We looked like we belonged there—like a couple of mice at a cat parade. After the host walked away, Jack cracked a funny joke and we both laughed. As we had been trained, when you're on surveillance, you do not want to look like law enforcement. The best way to do that is to laugh a lot. So, we do. Four men sat at a table on the other side of the room. Judging from their clothes, they looked like they just parked their camels at the curb. The men spoke Arabic in hushed tones. Jack nodded to me and I nodded back. Because they didn't speak English, Jack didn't have much to do other than think up the next joke. I took my powerful listening/recording device from my purse and placed it where it wouldn't be obvious. Standard procedure when doing surveillance of conversations is to use a listening and recording device which can pick up soft voices much better than the human ear. Later, we would listen to the words to see if there was anything interesting being said. I noticed one of the men staring at me, so I cracked a joke and Jack and I both laughed. Then I realized that the bastard was leering at me with a suggestive grin. I fantasized about smashing a beer bottle over his fucking head.

Jack and I spoke to each other with animated gestures,

another standard surveillance technique. So as not to block the words from the table we listened to, we spoke softly, often just moving our lips. Although we would learn a lot more when we listened to the recording later, I did pick up a few words. If I heard the word "bomb" once, I heard it a dozen times. I noticed that almost everyone in the restaurant was speaking Arabic. The place could have been in Yemen, not Oceanside, Long Island. If we go to this place again, which I think we will, I decided that I'd wear a burka to better blend in with the surroundings. A burka is more like a tent than an article of clothing. Jack says he thinks I'd look sexy in a burka. Always the delightful wiseass.

Our meal was served, which tasted horrible. I had ordered lamb with couscous and wild rice, and Jack ordered the same. I've never been a big fan of salt and pepper, but I couldn't put enough on my disgusting meal. After an hour we figured it was appropriate to leave. Jack handed the waiter his American Express card but was told they only accepted cash. Classy place. Fortunately, I had stopped at the bank earlier, so I had enough cash on me. Jack cracked one last joke and we walked out laughing.

When we got back to our house, Jack poured us a couple of martinis and we sat in the den to listen to our friendly gentlemen of the sand. After listening with me translating for a half-hour, we both wanted another martini. What we heard scared the hell out of us.

Chapter 35

After we listened to our recording from *Ali Island*, we called Rick Bellamy and asked that he meet us for breakfast at our place. We knew that Rick was working out of the Long Island office that day. Besides, Rick loves to come to our place. He and Ellen had visited us a few times and keep dropping hints for more invitations. Although Jack and I decided we would work by ourselves, after listening to the recording from *Ali Island* we both realized that it was time to roll out some heavy artillery, namely, Rick Bellamy.

At 8:30 a.m., Rick showed up with his assistant, Carol Longworth. Carol is one sharp agent and I was happy to see her. Sandy, bless her, had prepared a wonderful breakfast, a far cry from the shit we ate at *Ali Island* the day before. Sandy discreetly left the meeting room. She probably knew more about our conversation than we did, but she knew that Rick is a stickler for following procedure. After we ate, I flipped on my listening/recording device and hit play. It worked perfectly. We hardly missed a word, but I was the one who would do the translating. I had marked the passages that were most interesting so we wouldn't need to wade through a lot of Arabic chit chat.

"Here's the most interesting part," I said. "Listen carefully as I translate. The man speaking is Mustaffa Chudri, who, Carol tells us, is on the FBI Watch List."

Chudri spoke as I translated.

"We need to plan to detonate all the bombs within a short period of time. That won't give the infidels time to react. They will be drowning in a sea of violence."

"A sea of violence?" Holy shit. I put the recording on hold and distributed the photos I surreptitiously took of the men at the restaurant. Carol Longworth looked at them. The only one I had given her earlier was Mustaffa Chudri.

"Each and every one of these four guys is on the FBI Watch List," Carol said. "I'll write down the name of each of them on the back of the photos."

As I said, Carol is one sharp agent.

"So, we know who's involved," Rick Bellamy said, "and we know that they're all on our watch list. But we're missing something, something big."

"Yeah," I said, "we don't know where the bombs are or if they're armed. All that we know, according to Randy Jones, we're looking at a time frame of three months from now."

"We've got to move fast," Rick said.

"Problem is we don't know where we're going," Jack said.

Chapter 36

Jack and I decided that we didn't want to become frequent faces at the jihadi luncheonette, *Ali Island*. If we become identified as regular visiting infidels, we may as well resign ourselves to getting whacked. With Carol Longworth's help we put together a list of agents who would be tasked with visiting *Ali Island*. None of them will be required to speak or understand Arabic. Their only job would be to point the recording device at any diner who looked interesting. Carol passed the names by Rick, and he approved. The recording chips would be sent to me for translating.

So, according to Professor Randy Jones, we're looking at three months till show time. Not a comforting feeling to know that we may be soon under attack. But something was gnawing at me—the predicted timing. I decided to call Randy Jones.

"Hi, Randy, Becca Lang here. I hate to be a pain in the ass, but I have a big question. Do you feel comfortable with the prediction that the bomb attacks will occur in three months? What if our timing is off?"

"Becca, when dealing with jihadis I never feel comfortable with any predictions. Is it possible that the estimated timing was a piece of *disinformation* to throw us off? Yes, that's possible, and it won't be the first time we've been fed intentionally wrong information."

"So, it's accurate to say, Randy, that we're left guessing if we have the right timing."

"Yes, we're guessing. It could happen at any time."

Chapter 37

Shannon Bream for *Fox News*, ladies and gentlemen. I have an upsetting piece of breaking news to share with you. We have just received word that a bomb has been found at the Nassau Coliseum in Uniondale, Long Island. Although the information is still coming in, we believe that the bomb was a low yield nuclear device. A weapon like this is often referred to as a suitcase nuke because of its small size. The discovery occurred 20 minutes ago. We have no idea if other bomb plantings are in the works. We all owe our thanks to a sharp-eyed policeman who noticed the package in a spot where it shouldn't have been. All access roads to the coliseum site have been closed. Traffic in the area can only be described as a chaotic nightmare. Government vehicles have been dispatched to the site to monitor for radiation and to remove the weapon. Please avoid any roads leading to the Nassau Coliseum.

"Stay tuned to *Fox News* for updates on this story."

———

Rick Bellamy called a meeting at the FBI field office in Melville, Long Island. Jack and I will be there, along with

Professor Randy. As the saying goes, the shit has hit the fan. The big question in front of us is how much more shit is on the way, and where it's coming from.

Rick began the meeting by asking Professor Randy for his opinion as to what happened.

"What just happened is what we've all been afraid of," Randy said. "The bomb was planted two and a half months before the time we expected it. Thank God for that alert cop who noticed the package. But our national security can't depend on the good fortune of having a sharp-eyed cop on the scene. We find ourselves in the nasty position of pure guesswork. We have no idea when or if the next bomb planting will occur, or when it will happen."

"It's time to have a meeting with 'our friend' from Brooklyn," Bellamy said.

"Our friend?" all three of us asked.

"He's the deepest mole in the FBI," Rick said, "and that's why you folks don't know him. That changes right now. You all have top secret clearances, and now you have the sacred 'need to know' who 'our friend' is. His name is Muhammed Busharif, aka *Imam Mike*. He's the religious leader, or imam, of a mosque in Brooklyn. He's a trusted inside source, one of the best the FBI or the CIA has, if not *the* best. He gradually became infuriated with all of the terrorist killings in the name of his religion. When a good friend of his daughter was killed in a bomb attack at a football game, Mike went over the edge. He renounced his religion, but only to a select few people, including FBI Director Watson and me. Mike's language tends to be salty, not what you'd expect from a religious leader. Mike's on our side and is probably the most important mole we've ever had. Mike feeds us information that we could never get without an insider like him. Although he's not a professional, he operates like a seasoned spy. When he delivers a sermon in his mosque, he's careful to avoid any subject that's even mildly political. The last thing he can afford is to be labeled as 'a reformer.' He had an imam friend in Westchester, a reformer like himself, who would openly denounce the radicals in his sermons. The man is no longer among the living. Mike knows better. In his sermons he sticks to discussions of family matters, friendships, and religious observances. Mike knows how to remain invisible. He's also a good guy and easy to get along with. You'll like him. If anybody can give us a lead as to where the scumbags are hiding, it's Imam Mike. He will be here in a half hour."

Jack and I are gradually discovering that there is one hell of a lot that we *don't* know. We were both pissed off, to put it mildly, that Rick Bellamy hadn't told us about Professor Randy. And now we find out about "our friend," a guy who may be the key to the locked door of information, information that we need. Jack and I will definitely have a talk with Rick about this secrecy bullshit. I think Randy may want to be involved in the meeting.

Chapter 38

Jack and I sat in front of Rick Bellamy's desk, still furious that critical information had been kept from us.

At 2 p.m. we heard a knock on Rick Bellamy's door. Rick's assistant, Carol, led a Catholic priest into the office. The man was huge, about 6'4" I'd guess. He was slightly overweight, but mainly muscle. He had shoulders like a linebacker. We were expecting a Muslim cleric, but this guy was a priest, or at least that's the way he was dressed.

Rick introduced Randy, Jack, and me.

"Folks, meet Imam Muhammed Busharif, best known to us as Imam Mike. He prefers to be called Mike. As you can tell from the way he's dressed, Mike is fond of wearing disguises. As I told you a little while ago, Mike is our best inside mole, and now you guys have the privilege of meeting him."

I felt like slugging Rick in the nose. I mean shit, Jack and I should have had the "privilege" of meeting this guy Imam Mike a long time ago. Professor Randy should have known about him too. If Imam Mike was too far inside for us to know him, does that mean that we're too far outside? This secrecy is complete bullshit. Okay, time for a deep breath.

"Pleasure to meet you folks," Imam Mike said. "My dear friend, Rick Bellamy, has told me all about you, but that was only this morning. From what I just heard about you guys, I should have known about you before, and you should have known about me. I think Rick is a bit too strict about secrecy."

Randy, Jack, and I vigorously nodded our heads. I sensed that Rick Bellamy was embarrassed. He should be!

Mike continued. "I'm valuable to the FBI and CIA because of two things. I keep my mouth shut and my ears open. The jihadi slimeballs who attend my mosque are sometimes ridiculously open about their affairs, but not all the time. It's tough for me to keep my ears open when I don't know what I'm listening for. I've just learned that Professor Randy here has been completely on top of this bomb plot. Did anybody think to tell me so I could listen for that information? Rick, I've known you for a long time, and I don't think I'm being out of line when I say this excessive secrecy bullshit needs to stop."

I almost felt sorry for Rick. Almost. He's in the unenviable position of discovering that he's an asshole.

Imam Mike looked at me and began speaking in Arabic. We chatted in Arabic for a couple of minutes.

"I'm simply amazed that Dr. Becca here has learned Arabic in the past few months," Mike said. "It's not an easy language to learn, and Becca has managed to become fluent."

"I may be fluent," I said, "but a native speaker like yourself can pick up nuances that I may miss. I'm happy that I finally get to meet you, Mike, although until today I didn't know you existed." I stared at Rick Bellamy as I said that.

"I recommend that Becca and I become the translating

committee." Mike said. We exchanged a high five. Easy to like this guy. He then said a few words to me, none of which I even vaguely understood. It sounded like Arabic, but I didn't recognize one word.

Mike smiled and said, "As you noted, Becca, camel jockeys like me are good with language nuances."

"That's why we need to be on the same team, Mike," I said, drilling my eyes into Rick Bellamy.

Chapter 39

Rick Bellamy called a break, not just a bio break, but a break intended to let some of the steam out of the room. The percolating anger of Jack, Randy, and me created a tension in the room that would interfere with getting anything serious done. I just thank God that Imam Mike was in the meeting because his presence made it clear that the excessive secrecy was interfering with the FBI's simple friggin goal, which was to ward off terrorist attacks.

"Director Watson is here," Rick's assistant announced over the intercom.

Wow, Sarah Watson, Director of the FBI, would be in for the rest of our meeting. Neither Jack nor I had met her before, but had seen her many times on TV. She's a strikingly pretty woman in her late 50s, dressed to kill in an expensive business suit.

"During our break I asked Director Watson to attend our meeting," Rick Bellamy said. "She's in the New York office today. I filled her in on some of the tension that seems to have developed about my secrecy demands."

Director Watson, or Sarah as she insisted on being called,

had a look on her face that said, "I get it." She's well known for her sharp mind, attention to detail, and complete absence of bullshit.

"Please explain to these folks your thoughts on our secrecy demands, Sarah," Rick said. I think he was looking for a lifeline.

"Simply put, our secrecy protocols are off the charts in the wrong direction," Sarah said. "Rather than ensuring security, the protocols actually interfere with our mission. I've just met you folks for the first time, but I want to make something entirely clear. My colleague Rick Bellamy here is one of the finest agents our Bureau has ever produced. He explained to me that you guys are 'pissed off' as he put it, about our keeping secret the names of various of our agents, or in Imam Mike's case, 'our friend.' Please don't be angry with Rick. I'm here to tell you that these demands were mine, not Rick's. Yes, I'm the pain in the ass who complicates your lives. That stops right now. If I've learned anything over the years, it's to change course when you realize you're headed toward a brick wall, and that's exactly where I've been sending you folks. The reason for our tight secrecy protocols should be obvious, to keep a lid on security and make certain the enemy doesn't know what we're up to. But, from what Rick has told me, our secrecy demands have resulted in the left hand not knowing what the right hand is doing. Our colleague, Dr. Randy Jones, is one of the finest intellects on the subject of Islamic terrorism. And we kept it from you, Jack and Becca, and we kept you from him. Rick has convinced me that our secrecy protocols have resulted in the opposite of what we intended. That stops *now*. In retrospect it was a mistake, and when it comes to mistakes, I know what I'm doing—I stop making them. You all have top secret clearances, but from this day forward I hereby announce that you all have the precious 'need to know' everything about our antiterrorist operation, yes, *everything*. No more guessing. You will have the answers and the ability to get answers when you need them. I repeat, this was my call, not Rick Bellamy's. I hope I've cleared the air on this bullshit. Any questions or comment? Dr. Lang?"

"Please call me Becca. Jack and I often share the same thoughts, and I know that I'm speaking for the two of us when I say that we're delighted with what you've said today. Yes, we were feeling left out of critical information, but your comments have put an end to that. I'm happy that you cleared Rick Bellamy, a man for whom we have nothing but respect."

"I'm happy to hear you say that, Becca. I now have some startling news for all of you, including you, Rick. You are about to hear it from me first."

She poured herself a glass of water from the pitcher. As I had always heard about Sarah Watson, she has a talent for introducing drama into a conversation. And that's what she just did.

"That bomb plot was not a plot at all, it was a hoax," Sarah said as she put down her glass.

Holy shit, am I hearing this right? The friggin bomb plot was a hoax?

Sarah continued. "Just before coming here I got word from the bomb squad that not only was there no nuclear materials in the weapon, it wasn't a weapon at all. That's right, it looked like a bomb but it wasn't a bomb. It was just a hunk of metal and a bunch of wires. I know that you and Jack got the warning from your translation of what you heard at that terrorist hotbed, the *Ali Island* restaurant. I'm now asking Imam Mike to comment on that."

"Yes, Sarah, the *Ali Island* is a constant source of information—*DISINFORMATION*. If I was in communication with Becca and Jack, I would have alerted them to that little tidbit of knowledge. It seems that the jihadis simply assume they are being spied on and spout lies to throw us off the scent. It doesn't surprise me at all that the bomb was a hoax."

Jack and I looked at each other. Then I turned to Sarah.

"It's a creepy feeling to learn that you've been duped, Sarah, but it appears that is exactly what happened to Jack and me."

"Yes, Jack and you, as well as Dr. Jones here, as well as Rick Bellamy, as well as me. We've all been duped. Jack, you have a comment?"

"So, we've been working with the wrong information, *disinformation*. We're suddenly faced with a question. Now what?"

"Let's take a short break," Sarah said. "I may need to throw up before I hit you with the next announcement."

Chapter 40

After our break, I couldn't help but notice that Sarah's pretty, calm face looked constricted. When she walked back into the room, she stopped in front of my chair and narrowed her gaze on me. *On me?* What's *that* about? I'd find out soon enough.

Sarah stood at the front of the room.

"So, we're all sitting here thinking that we dodged a bullet. But we now know that the bullet was a blank. What I'm about to tell you may get you physically ill. In the past day, from our hundreds of inside sources, we've found out something that's almost too horrible to think about."

She paused a moment and took another sip of water. Hey, enough with the emotional foreplay. What the hell are we facing?

"In a word, epidemic," Sarah said. "Yes, epidemic, or more likely a pandemic, which is a worldwide epidemic. We've received information that a group in Yemen is planning to spread a virus to all countries, that's right *all* countries. As of now, we don't have much information on the virus, but we do know that there is no antidote or vaccine."

She walked over to where I was sitting and looked at me again. Now I realized what her gaze was all about after the break. Oh my God, I don't think I want to hear this.

"Becca, the hour has come and you're the woman of the hour. It's well known that you're the nation's expert on epidemics and pandemics. Hell, you wrote a paper that is the standard reference source for information on spreading viruses. Your *New England Journal of Medicine* article has put you on the map, my friend. I wish you and Jack could relax in that beautiful new waterfront house of yours, but the alarm is about to sound, and you're the one to answer it. I read about your courageous actions when you were a Navy doctor in Afghanistan, and how you saved your military facility from being overrun by a modern-day plague. What we're faced with is worse, a lot worse. Shortly, you will be hearing from the White House, from President Matt Blake himself. God bless you, Becca. God bless all of us."

Jack looked at me and flashed a smile, a smile that reminded me that he's always there for me. I can do without Jack as easy as I can do without oxygen. To get my mind off the shit I just heard, all I wanted to think about was soaking in our hot tub and making love under the stars. Looks like life has other plans for us.

Chapter 41

It's him, honey."

"Him, meaning whom?"

"President Blake."

"Good evening, Mr. President."

"Becca, so nice to speak to you again. The last time we talked was when I called you in Afghanistan to congratulate you on successfully defeating a virus at Bagram Airfield. I know this call isn't a surprise. Sarah Watson told me she has explained the situation to you."

Typical of my nutty Type A personality, I had already begun to get on the case before the President called.

"Yes, sir, she has. I've already been in touch with the CDC and have started to map out a plan. This will be a huge and complex operation, sir, but the faster we work, the better our chance of success."

"Please define success, Becca."

"Survival."

"The country is counting on you, Becca. Actually, the world is counting on you. Thank God we have the best person for the job. You will be hearing regularly from Mike Prentiss, my Chief of Staff. Mike has an amazing way of keeping on top of things, just like you."

"Godspeed, my friend. Godspeed."

Yes, Godspeed. Ouch.

"Jack, honey, come here please. I need a hug."

"Shouldn't we be wearing masks?"

I cracked up.

"Keep the jokes coming, baby. We're going to need them."

So, we're faced with a pandemic and your humble doctor is in charge of staving it off. Yes, Sarah Watson officially announced that I'm the director of our war against killer microbes. I couldn't have been happier that Sarah Watson decided to do an about-face on the FBI habit of secrecy, and Jack felt the same way. The major thing we need with what we may be confronted with is information, a steady flow of information, without bowing to the altar of "need to know." We have one important set of circumstances on our side— the virus hasn't been turned loose yet. All of our information comes from inside intelligence, and because of Sarah Watson's newfound change on the issue of secrecy, intelligence is our best friend—at this point, our only friend.

After I got off the phone with President Blake, I got a call from Mike Prentiss, his Chief of Staff. Mike said that the administration would prefer that I work out of the White

House. Bullshit, although I didn't put it so bluntly. If I'm in charge, I'm just that—*in charge*. We can easily arrange to have TV cameras installed in our house for my regular appearances. Although I haven't put the protocols in place yet, one of the most essential is to simply stay where the hell you are unless it's absolutely necessary to leave. Among the many chores I need to accomplish, keeping myself alive is one of them.

I realized early on that one of the most important ingredients in our war is to come up with a list of protocols and procedures to follow. There is one person who I need help from in putting together a working manual—Jack. He's the smartest person I've ever met, and I trust his judgment like I trust that the sun will rise in the East. We sat down with Seth and Sandy and flat out asked them if they were okay with being quarantined, and not leaving the house. As I expected, they both agreed. I then asked them, as Jack and I had discussed, if they thought I should offer living quarters to Randy, Sandy's dad. They both enthusiastically agreed, and opined that Randy would love the idea. They love and respect Randy, and welcomed the idea of watching out for him, especially after Sandy's mom died. God knows we have the room, and I can use his vast knowledge to help us with our task. At our invitation, Randy Jones moved into his suite at our house. He seemed really happy with his new waterfront location.

As usual, I awoke early. I walked into the kitchen where Sandy was preparing breakfast. "Hi, honey, what's new?" I asked.

She flashed a huge smile at me. "Dad's in love. You and Jack are the perfect matchmakers. He wants to marry Molly Pearson, and I think she's good with the idea too. I couldn't be happier for my 44-year old widower dad. He's been lonely as hell since mom died, and when he met Molly at your house the other day, I could see that something in his brain clicked big-time, and I noticed that hers did too.

Randy walked in and sat at the counter.

"So, Randy, it seems that you've been carousing around after my pretty neighbor," my wiseass mouth cracked.

"I sure have been. I proposed marriage last night and she accepted."

"My God, Dad, you work fast."

"Things move along rapidly when you're in your mid 40s like Molly and me. Becca, I can't thank you and Jack enough for inviting me to live here, and Molly loves the idea too.

I felt confident that I was surrounded by people who would help me get the job done. Jack, Randy, Sandy, and Seth, and soon Molly, my smart, funny neighbor. *My cabinet, my Bayfront Gang.*

The only person missing was Rachel, my BFF. But we'd talk regularly on the phone.

Jack insisted on cooking dinner tonight. We invited Molly, of course, who brought a couple of suitcases with her to move into Randy's suite. For a guy with an Adonis body, Jack sure as hell knows how to make a mean pasta dish. When he cooks, I remind myself to run and work out the next day to keep the calories in control. Tonight, he prepared stuffed shells with

Ricotta cheese, shrimp and chicken, preceded with a tasty salad. As we finished eating, Jack posed a question.

"Becca and I think we have an excellent plan outlined, thanks in large part to input from you guys. But something is missing. Anyone care to guess?"

"What's missing is any evidence of the virus itself," Randy said. "All of our discussions are based on intelligence that we've gathered, but the actual event has yet to happen."

"Could it be that we've been fed yet another round of disinformation?" Sandy said.

"A non-event is something I think we'd all love," I interjected, "but I don't think that will be the outcome. Randy's research, including the information he's gotten from his hordes of insiders, is pretty solid. And it's backed by data from the FBI and the CIA. The really positive thing is that we're more prepared than we would be without the research. I've convinced the White House to put into play the necessary plans, including the wearing of facemasks, hand washing, and social distancing. If the virus hits, we're ready to go."

"But we have no idea what the virus consists of, nor do we know the symptoms, not to mention the morbidity and mortality rate," Randy said. "I think we could be in for some horrifying times. And we have no idea when the horror will start."

"Let's think positively," Molly said, as she reached over and squeezed Randy's hand, "which is easy for me with my new honey over here. Becca, Jack, I just want you to know I'm part of your team. Just tell me what to do and I'll get it done. I feel like I just acquired a new family."

It's easy to like Molly, or *Miss Molly* as I love to call her.

Typical of her, she stepped right up to the plate to let us know she was aboard. Professor Molly is one sharp cookie.

Randy and Molly announced that they'd like to get married. But, because of the looming pandemic, traveling outside *Bayfront* is forbidden, even though the virus hasn't launched yet. Yes, it was my call, but everybody agreed. I called Father Guzman who said no problem. He'd conducted *"Zoom"* weddings before. So, in our beautiful den with Father Guzman on the TV in front of us, Randy and Molly took their vows. Jack was Randy's best man and I served as Molly's maid of honor. A real 21st Century wedding. Jack dragged out the booze and Seth placed himself at the piano, cranking out one Gershwin hit after another, music that Randy and Molly love. Jack and I stared into each other's eyes. Our little "family" was growing. The only one missing was my BFF Rachel, but we still manage to speak on the phone every day.

I'm scheduled for the first of my constant TV appearances the next day. Sandy and Molly, my crack research team, prepared me for the interview. Tonight, I'm scheduled to be interviewed on *CBS Evening News*. It will not be a pleasant interview. I hate to say it, but I'm becoming talented at seeing the shit heading toward the fan.

Chapter 42

Good evening ladies and gentlemen, I'm Norah O'Donnell for *CBS Evening News*. I'm afraid that I'm going to upset you this evening with a horrifying breaking news story. For months we've been hearing rumors about a possible viral epidemic that could go worldwide as a pandemic. The government has done nothing to quash the rumors, the thinking being that we should prepare ourselves for what may come. Well, it has come, and it's terrifying.

We have just received reports that Lisbanta, a small town of 10,000 people near Lisbon, Portugal, has become infected with a rapidly spreading virus. The original news came just 12 hours ago. As of today, 6,000 people have died within a 24-hour period. That's 60 percent of the town, an amazing and shocking number. And it's only just begun. The disease hits without warning, and there is no known vaccine or antidote for it. The symptoms are immediate and shocking. People who have contracted the disease show immediate symptoms of acute respiratory distress, often gasping for air, and death comes within hours.

I have with us, via satellite hookup, Dr. Rebecca Lang, a Lieutenant Commander in the Naval Reserve and a former combat physician at Bagram Airbase in Afghanistan. Dr. Lang, or Becca as she prefers to be called, is recognized by many to be the world's leading experts on epidemics and pandemics. She wrote an article in *The New England Journal of Medicine* that has become the recognized source for information on these dreaded diseases. Just so you know, a pandemic is nothing more than an epidemic, except it is worldwide in scope. President Blake has asked Dr. Lang to lead our country's fight against this contagion. Dr. Lang, please give us your take on this shocking story."

"Good evening, Norah, and please call me Becca. As you accurately noted, this story doesn't come as a surprise. We've been expecting to hear about this virus for months, and that's the good news, if there *is* any good news. Although we have no vaccine for the disease, we do have in place procedures and protocols for slowing its spread, and the United States has shared its knowledge with the rest of the world. You all heard about the danger of a rapidly spreading virus with the worldwide Coronavirus, the Covid 19 pandemic, a few years ago. That contagion eventually came to an end with the discovery of a vaccine.

"The White House is calling this looming pandemic the Portuguese Virus, because that is where it was first discovered. So far, this virus appears to be much more severe than Covid 19, and its symptoms are worse. One of the truly startling things about this Portuguese Virus is that it infects people of all age groups and physical condition. Yes, it's infected children and young adults as viciously as it attacks elderly people. Norah, I implore you to help us sound the alarm as you are now doing with the words at the bottom of the TV screen.

1. Wear a mask

2. Maintain a distance of six feet between yourself and

anyone else. This is known as personal or social distancing.

3. Wash your hands regularly with soap and water for at least 20 seconds, more often if you have been in contact with anybody.

4. Stay home. That's easier to say than to enforce. Some people are required by their jobs to be out in the community. But, if at all possible, work from home, using computer technology.

"I cannot overemphasize the importance of following these guidelines," I said. "Voluntary compliance is absolutely necessary. I'm asking all your viewers to please consider it your *personal responsibility* to keep the virus from spreading. President Blake has asked me to take charge of this war, and make no doubt about it, it is a war, a war against invisible microbes. I will be reporting daily on TV with the latest news in a White House press briefing. We're in the early stages of this crisis. If we all take it upon ourselves to personally fight this contagion, we will succeed. But again, I emphasize that we all need to take personal responsibility. Thank you, and I'll be reporting to you regularly."

My "gang," led by Jack, gave me a round of applause after my TV appearance. That was sweet, but my stomach was in a friggin knot. Seth, in addition to his many talents, is quite the expert at handling audiovisual equipment. I was happy to see that, because it would require one less visit from an outsider. Oh, dear Lord, I'm beginning to think of anyone who doesn't live here as an "outsider."

Chapter 43

Like many people, when there's a crisis I suffer from a thing called *News Fear*. Yes, I find myself fearful of turning on the morning news, either radio or TV, especially when I hold a leadership position in fighting the crisis. But, because of my incredible team consisting of Jack, Sandy and Seth Lightfoot, Randy Jones, and now Molly, I know the news before it hits the airwaves. Molly is one hell of a fast researcher, and feeds me information before it gets to the networks. Sandy works right there with her. And what I've learned has me nauseated. I turned on the TV and tuned to *Fox News* for the morning show, *Fox and Friends*. I had met one of the anchors, Brian Kilmeade, a few years ago. I respect his intelligence and his sense of humor, and I think of him as a friend. I wanted to hear what he had to report, although I already knew the facts, the horrifying facts. I had just received a call from the producer, and they want to include my daily White House report for this morning's broadcast. Jack handed me the latest research, mainly from Sandy and Molly.

"Brian Kilmeade for *Fox and Friends*, ladies and gentlemen. We know that a lot of our viewers like to tune to *Fox and Friends* for our often light-hearted treatment of breaking news stories, But this morning I have nothing light to report to you. Instead

I have a horrifying story to tell you about. Yesterday we heard that what's become known as the Portuguese Virus, or Pvirus, had infected the town of Lisbanta in Portugal, and that no less than 6,000 people, that's 60 percent of the town's inhabitants died. I'm about to report the most terrifying piece of news I've ever had to deliver. As of today, that's 24 hours after the virus was first reported, all of the residents of Lisbanta have perished, yes 100 percent. The town has been wiped out."

The camera panned away from Kilmeade, who was wiping tears and sweat from his face. When the camera once again got Kilmeade on the air, he had managed to compose himself as best he could.

"We are about to tune into a news conference from the White House, which is connected to Doctor Rebecca Lang, a good friend of mine, via live newsfeed. Dr. Lang is also a Lieutenant Commander in the Naval Reserve. President Blake has recently appointed her as our nation's leader and spokesperson on this terrible pandemic. I say pandemic, because that's what it is, a worldwide epidemic. Dr. Lang is the author of an article published in the past few years in *The New England Journal of Medicine* on the subject of spreading viruses. It is widely recognized as the most accurate source of information on the subject. I bring you now to the White House."

I had just gotten off the phone with the White House. President Blake himself spoke to me with Mike Prentiss, his Chief of Staff, sitting next to him. They both told me what I already knew. Yes, report the facts as I know them, but avoid any words that could lead to panic. Easier said than done, given what I'd just learned. But the last thing I wanted to do was downplay the seriousness of the problem we're facing. No way in hell can we as a nation tolerate college frat parties thumbing their noses at the crisis without any steps to prevent the spread of the virus. Rather than spend an hour going down a rapidly changing list of cities that have become infected, I chose to simply list those few areas where the virus hadn't yet hit. Sandy sat next to me with her laptop, bringing me the latest information. Seth had put together a chart that we would show regularly, a chart not emphasizing the areas that were hit, but rather a chart of what absolutely must be done defensively.

"Thank you, Brian, and thank you, Mr. President," I said, "and good morning my fellow Americans. This morning I'm going to share with you the facts as we know them as of right now, but the most important part of my comments are the *positive steps* we can all take to put a stop to this crisis."

I showed a chart listing the most seriously affected American cities as well as cities worldwide. In the United States, Seattle was the hardest hit, followed by Baltimore, New York, Los Angeles, and Houston. I had a sickening feeling that I was playing a deadly serious game. The virus is so fast moving and widespread that showing affected areas doesn't tell the real story. I decided I'd get everyone's attention by hitting them with the most troubling fact of all—the amazing speed of the spreading virus.

"Folks, let's focus on the most troubling of all the statistics. Two days ago, the Portuguese Virus, now known as the Pvirus, was a theory, a set of predictions of what may occur. Only yesterday we received the news about Lisbanta, a small town in Portugal with a population of only 10,000 people. We were all shocked that 60 percent of the residents died in the first day. Now, as Brian Kilmeade reported this morning, we learn that 100 percent of the residents of that sad town have perished. That statistic shows two things: first the rapid spread of the disease, but the most important thing about Lisbanta is this. It has become known that the leadership of the town didn't take any necessary steps even in light of the dire predictions. The major newspaper in the town carried an editorial three days ago, written by the town mayor himself, decrying the predictions as fearmongering, and made light of the warnings, but most important of all, made light of precautionary steps that could have been taken. So, the steps were not taken, and tragedy resulted. Let's take a look at what steps we can all take—*right now*—to avoid a repeat of Lisbanta. You are about to see on your screen the necessary steps we all need to take. To get a copy of this document, visit www.whitehouse.gov/pvirussteps. I'm showing you the steps now, along with some added commentary from me:

1. Wear a mask whenever you're among people. Don't think about it, don't say that it's uncomfortable or annoying, just do it. It's something we're all going to need to live with—or die without. A mask not only protects you from being infected, it protects others from you. Keep a supply of clean masks handy at all times, and don't even think about venturing forth without your mask.

2. Maintain a distance of six feet between yourself and anyone else. This is known as personal or social distancing. It's easy to do. Just as with wearing masks, don't think about it, just do it.

3. Wash your hands regularly with soap and water for at least 20 seconds, more often if you have been in contact with anybody.

4. Stay home. That's easier to say than to do. Some people are required by their jobs to be out in the community. But, if at all possible, work from home, using the Internet. Our modern computer technology has given us tools we

didn't have just a few short years ago.

5. Accept personal responsibility. Don't for an instant think that these rules are just for others to follow. No, they're for you—and me—to follow.

"To the extent that we follow these rules and accept personal responsibility, is the extent to which we can defeat this virus. Thank you, and we'll be talking again soon."

Randy, Molly, Sandy, and Seth cheered loudly after my appearance. Jack, of course, hugged me. I walked over to the piano which was 20 feet away from the TV camera. I put my hand on the piano and said,

"Hey, Seth, how about some ragtime?"

I was clear as hell that taking personal responsibility also meant taking responsibility for our attitudes, which may as well be positive. We need to lighten up.

Seth got it, and played some of the best rag I'd ever heard. Randy and Molly danced an old time Savoy. Jack and I joined in. I always think of myself as a klutz when it comes to dancing, but I'm committed that our lives will include a little lighthearted fun.

If at all possible.

Chapter 44

So, President Blake has appointed me the point lady of this entire fucking mess. But, although I've been given considerable power, no way will I assert that power at *Bayfront*. We've become like a tight-knit little family—*The Bayfront Gang*—and I wasn't about to bark orders. We reach decisions by agreement, not by my commands, although everybody respectfully listens to me.

Ever since I met and fell in love with him in Afghanistan, I knew that Jack is a born leader, yes a *born* leader. It's just in him. Although he pushed back, I convinced him that he would be our leader at *Bayfront,* and he would call meetings, not me. Of course, he would always touch base with me before making a decision. He has one of the most important traits of a leader—he has humility.

We kept in regular touch with my folks, a mile away in East Islip, and with Jack's in Mamaroneck. I also called Jack's sister, Rachel, my BFF, once a day.

We agreed to a few *Bayfront* rules, or guidelines. Because we quarantined ourselves, we would not wear masks unless one of us needed to go out, say for supplies. Seth, bless him, insisted that he be the "supply guy," and would be the one to run errands and to pick up supplies. Avoiding restaurants and taverns was easy because I had issued a rule, backed by Congress and the White House, that no restaurants could open, including outdoor restaurants. Did I feel responsible for putting tens of thousands of good people out of work? Yes, I did. It's a shitty feeling, but staying alive sometimes requires making shitty decisions.

When I did the research for my *New England Journal of Medicine* article on epidemics and pandemics, I learned an immutable rule for any virus—It takes time to learn what you're dealing with. And we were learning about the Pvirus more every day. In my public addresses I would try to avoid sounding negative, but my God, we are faced with the scariest disease imaginable. That a town of 10,000 in Portugal could be totally wiped out in two days was the scariest fact about the virus, and the news each day didn't make it any less scary.

Sandy and Molly appointed themselves, with the full agreement of me and Jack, as the Internet research gurus. They would pass their research by Randy before handing it to me. They would give me my announcements each day before my White House press briefing. They would take turns getting up real early (5 a.m.) so that I would have the latest news before it hit the networks. Because of my position, we had access to government sites that weren't available to the public. Sandy and Molly had a tough job and performed it perfectly.

Seth hooked up the TV camera and audio equipment.

Today's major announcement was that the Navy's newest and largest aircraft carrier, the *USS Gerald R. Ford,* has been hit with the Pvirus as she steamed in the Azores. She carries a crew of 4,539, including the airwing. As of this morning, fully half of the crew had died, including the captain. Admiral Walter Franken, The Chief of Naval Operations, whom I introduced at the briefing, ordered the ship to head toward one of the islands and drop anchor. Without saying, it, the Admiral Franken's thinking was obvious. What if the entire crew perished? No way could we have a nuclear aircraft carrier steaming the seas without a crew manning it.

I felt like popping a Maalox to calm my screaming stomach. But, as Jack and I agreed, it was best to avoid medications. Instead I took deep breaths and used some of my Eastern meditation practices. Keeping my own shit together is one of my highest priorities.

Next, I reported the latest American cities to be afflicted. The numbers can only be described as staggering. Houston, one of the worst hit in terms of percentages, was a perfect example of the word *staggering*. In three days, 25 percent of the city's 2.3 million citizens had died, and 30 percent more had been infected.

Jack handed me a tall glass of ice water after I finished my White House briefing. Truth be told, I would have preferred gin. I sat in the den with my gang.

"I know I should show you guys a stiff upper lip, but the numbers we're seeing are absolutely horrifying. Molly, as a history professor, imagine that you're writing an article a year from now. What would be the title of the article?"

"The Extinction of the Human Race."

Chapter 45

Molly is one straight-shooting lady, not given to dramatic exaggeration. When she said she contemplated the extinction of humanity, she scared the shit out of me, not that it was her intention. Hell, as the nation's leading expert on pandemics, I know a lot about this stuff, not just statistics but the medical science behind viruses. And Molly's right. Unless we can get a handle on what's happening, we're looking at exactly that—mass extinction.

Jack and I sat on the deck having coffee. When I need to get my mind working, sitting and talking with Jack always does the trick. My God, is he smart. That I'm crazy in love with him is a nice bonus.

"So, what are you thinking, Jack, after Molly's scary announcement?"

"Enzymes."

"Enzymes? Please explain, baby."

"Well, as we know, an enzyme is a biological catalyst that accelerates chemical reactions. It's like an additive to fuel, making things happen fast or faster. One of the stocks I've been researching for my day trades is called Accelero, or

ACCE on NASDAQ. The company has just discovered a new enzyme, Delta 560, which is one ass-kicking catalyst. It's similar to trypsin, an enzyme that is produced in the pancreas. The reason the market loves it is because the enzyme rapidly accelerates any chemical reaction to which it's introduced. So, my speculation is that if this stuff is matched up with the ingredients of the killer virus, that may explain the rapid spread. And no way in hell is this a work of nature. No, some group is behind all of this."

"Dear God, Jack, I love when you speculate with that big brain of yours. I'm calling the CDC right now and turn them loose on this idea. I'm scheduled to speak to them today, anyway. They have a normal bureaucratic resistance to outside input, but they listen to me. And I listen to *you*."

The landline phone rang and Sandy picked it up. Our house rule for answering the phone is simple. If it's near you when it rings, pick it up.

"Dr. Rebecca Lang's Office (our agreed-upon way of answering the phone), Sandra Lightfoot speaking, how may I help you?"

"Becca, it's a Dr. Maxwell Morton from the CDC for you. He said he's returning your call," Sandy said, handing me the phone.

"Becca, good to hear your voice, my friend. I think your morning briefings with the White House are great, if somewhat scary."

"Hey, Max, I have an idea that I'd like your geniuses at CDC to track down. According to my husband, Jack (who says hello by the way), there is a new fast-acting enzyme called Delta 560. It's just a hunch, but our hunches are pretty good, especially Jack's. As we well know, the most amazing thing about this Pvirus is the incredible speed at which it spreads. A fast-acting enzyme is one way to make that happen."

"As usual, Becca, you're way ahead of us. I repeat my constant plea. After this crisis is over I want you to consider working for the CDC. I'm thinking of retiring, and I can't think of a better person to replace me as Director. My God, can we use your big brain here. I'm going to refer Jack's enzyme idea to Dr. Jennifer Clarke, a scientist with whom we work. She's located in our Washington D.C. office. Jenny is married to an Army general who works at the Pentagon. Here's her number."

It was after six, but what the hell, the Pvirus doesn't keep normal hours.

"Harry Clarke, may I help you?"

"Colonel Clarke, is that you? This is Becca Lang."

"Becca, my old friend. I'm proud to announce that I'm now a Lieutenant General. I've been meaning to call you. My fiancée, Jennifer, who I'm happy to say is now my wife, gave me that book that you and Captain Jack wrote. She gave it to me for my birthday before we got married. As she admits, Jenny is a hopeless romantic, and my God what a wonderful romance your book is. An amazing and true love story. I was happy to see that you didn't portray me in the book as the asshole I sometimes can be."

"Don't be silly, Harry. I would never think of you as an asshole. A pain in the ass, maybe, but never an asshole. Jack's right here, I'll put him on speaker."

"Jack, honey, it's Colonel Clarke, who is now General Clarke. He wants to say hello."

"Hi, Jack. I was just telling Becca how much I loved your book. I'm delighted that my Afghanistan friends are now happily married. Please call me Harry."

"Good to talk to you, Harry, and congratulations on your promotion. What a coincidence that Becca has some big stuff to talk to your wife about."

"Becca always has big stuff to talk about. Our nation is lucky to have her in charge of fighting this goddam virus. Becca did one hell of a job in Afghanistan. I don't think I'm telling you anything you don't know, but I was pretty smitten with the beautiful lady who became your wife. You beat me to the punch, you handsome dog. Let me put Jenny on. Good talking to you, Jack."

"Hi, this is Jenny Clarke. Max Morton told me to expect your call and told me a bit about your ideas."

"Hi, Jenny, Becca Lang here. Jack is still on speaker. Because the enzyme idea was his, he should be part of our conversation. After God created Jack, he threw away the book on IQ statistics."

"I think your enzyme suspicions are brilliant," Jenny said. "I don't know why I didn't think of that myself, but I'm not Becca—or Jack. I'll turn my people loose on this tomorrow and keep you posted on what we find. The CDC folks in Atlanta work fast, and Doctor Max is a terrific scientist. Let's keep our fingers crossed. If I may suggest, Becca, I recommend that you don't include our conversation in your White House briefing tomorrow."

"I won't go into detail, of course, but the President wants me to include in my remarks anything positive. Shit, after the statistics I've put out in the past few days, the nation needs something positive to think about. I'll just say that the CDC is working on some new ideas. That alone should give people some confidence. We'll talk soon, Jenny."

I felt good after speaking with Jenny Clarke. Max Morton told me all about her. He couldn't be happier to hire her at the CDC, based on her well-known published works on disease control. That she's married to my old military boss was a fun bonus fact. According to Max, she has a reputation for working fast and accurately, happy words to my ears.

With the alarming rate that the Pvirus is coming down on us, speed is important.

Sandy is preparing dinner tonight, a seafood medley, a lot of which we caught right off our dock. Our "family" dinners are becoming more and more important to me. Keeping up morale with *The Bayfront Gang* is a key ingredient in keeping our heads screwed on. We have definitely become a family, a small tight family. We care about each other, a lot. We've become united in solving a problem none of us could have imagined possible a short time ago—saving the human race.

Chapter 46

I t's 6 a.m. and Molly and Sandy are preparing me for my talk to the nation via the White House news feed. Jack and I, as well as the rest of *The Bayfront Gang*, have disciplined ourselves to maintain a positive attitude during the shit we're putting up with. Today will be my fourth briefing, and my stomach was feeling anything but positive.

"Good morning, my fellow Americans. I wish I had some good news for you, but I don't. As we reported yesterday, the *USS Gerald R. Ford,* the world's largest aircraft carrier, has been hit by the Pvirus, hit hard. Yesterday we reported that fully half of the crew, including the captain, came down with the virus and died. At the order of the Chief of Naval Operations, the *Ford* dropped anchor off Sao Miguel Island in the Azores. Today, the news is worse. The entire crew of the *Ford* has perished. Yes, every human being aboard is dead. The proud carrier is now a floating tomb."

As I spoke a video was displayed showing the gigantic ship at anchor, a lifeless vessel that included 4,539 dead bodies. I switched off my voice feed and put in the code that hooked me up to the producer. I ordered him to remove the live video of the *Ford*. I decided it was too sickening to look at. He readily agreed.

I then addressed the virus attacks on American cities.

"Yesterday, we reported that Houston, Texas, was hit hard by the disease, and today the story is even worse. Fully 90 percent of Houston's citizens have died from the virus. The following cities have seen over 50 percent of their populations infected: Atlanta, Chicago, Minneapolis, and New York."

I took a sip of water that Jack just handed to me.

"*The Symphony of the Seas*, the world's largest cruise ship, was en route to its homeport in Los Angeles when the virus hit. Although we don't have the latest tally, we are told that 6,000 of the 6,600 passengers aboard have died. The ship has dropped anchor off Los Angeles. Port officials will not allow the ship into the Port of Los Angeles. The ship will remain at anchor in quarantine for one month. According to the trade group, Cruise Lines International Association (CLIA), 75 ships were at sea from American, Bahamian, and Caribbean ports alone when the virus hit. And I'm not counting ships from European and Asian nations. Those ships are now stranded at sea. Because of the extreme contagiousness and rapid spread, one affected passenger can inflict the disease on an entire ship. I've just been handed a report (from Sandy and verified by Molly and Randy) that the Cunard Line ship, the Queen Mary II (QMII), has been hit with the virus and is currently steaming near Puerto Rico. I don't yet have any information on the number of passengers and crew who may have become infected. That's all for my report today. I'll be bringing you another update tomorrow."

Chapter 47

Hecka hecka hecka, do the funky Becca."

Seth had launched into goofy mode and wrote one crazy song after another. I loved what he was doing. As stupid as the lyrics of his songs were, they all helped answer a simple question—How to lighten up our somber moods.

Randy declared a "bar joke war," and we all agreed to engage in the battle.

"A horse walks into a bar," Randy said. "Why the long face? the bartender asked."

We all cracked up.

"A hackneyed cliché walks into a bar feeling fit as a fiddle," Molly said.

"A typo walks into a *bra* and says, 'Your point is well-*maid*,'" Sandy weighed in.

"A homophone walks into a bar and says, 'Please put my beer *their*. Is it okay if I sit *hear*?'" Jack contributed.

"A split infinitive walks into a bar to boldly go where he

has not gone before," Seth recommended.

"An overused adverb walks into a bar, quickly crosses the room, enthusiastically orders a frizzly drink, and downs it hurriedly," I said.

We were having a blast. God bless Randy for his *bar joke war*.

The house phone rang and Molly picked up.

"It's Jenny Clarke from the CDC for you, Becca."

I stopped laughing and took a deep breath.

"I've put the line on speaker, Jenny. Jack is listening in."

"Jack's enzyme speculation is fabulous," Jenny said. "My people have been at it all morning. The White House had information that the enzyme Jack mentioned may have originated in Yemen. I've contacted the CIA to track down that possibility. If we know where the enzyme came from, we may be able to figure out a way to combat it. You may want to weigh in with the CIA. My contact is none other than Gamal Akhbar, aka George Atkins, better known as Buster, the Director of the CIA. We'll talk again soon."

My God, none other than Buster, the most ass-kicking director the CIA ever had. Jack and I had met him once at the White House and had a long lunch with him, striking up a friendship. He's a charming, friendly guy, but make no mistake about it, Buster gets the job done, no matter how big the job. He's a Coptic Christian, his parents hailing from Lebanon. He's well known for his ongoing war with radical Islam. "I'm a jihadi's worst nightmare," Buster would say. "I look like them and I talk like them, but I'm not one of them. I hunt them down and kill them." Unlike most CIA directors,

Buster came up through the ranks as a spy. His predecessor referred to Buster as a "super spook." Buster is well known as a man who, as he puts it, "takes no shit."

Jack and I were thrilled that Buster is "on the case." We placed a call to the CIA.

"Director Atkins, please. Dr. Rebecca Lang here."

"Becca, good to hear from you, my friend. How is Jack?" "Jack's right here on speaker. Is this line secure, Buster?"

"Of course, it's secure. Hey, you're speaking to *spook central*. Hi, Jack. Always a pleasure to talk to a genuine war hero. Let me take a guess. You folks are calling about the CDC research on that elusive enzyme, the one we think originates in my favorite terrorist hotbed, Yemen. Since this goddam virus crisis started, we at the CIA have basically memorized your article about pandemics in *The New England Journal of Medicine*, Becca. President Blake sure knew what he was doing when he put you in charge of this mess. You're the smartest doctor to roam the earth."

"Coming from a guy like you, I take that as a special compliment. So, listen, Buster, is there anything you can tell us about that Delta 560 enzyme? You mentioned that you've determined that it originates in Yemen. Anything more at this point?"

"No, but we've only just begun," Buster said. "But there's one thing that's odd. If this enzyme is in any way connected to the Pvirus, why haven't we seen cases of people coming down with the disease in Yemen? So far, our insiders tell us there's no evidence of it."

"Buster," I said, "I assume you know a man commonly referred to as Imam Mike."

"Of course, Mike is the best insider that the CIA and FBI has. I think it's time we had a conference call with him. He prefers to meet us in person wearing one of his disguises, but this goddam pandemic forces us to change our normal way of doing things. We've managed to get him a phone that is completely secure. I know that he's at a conference today. Let's plan on talking to him tomorrow after your scary White House briefing."

Chapter 48

My White House televised briefing today won't be any less scary than my previous ones, maybe even more so. Every major city in the country has become infected, and the deaths are piling up like lumber. So as not to appear like an undertaker at each of my briefings, I ordered a chart to be shown at the bottom of the screen with the cities scrolling by, without my reciting the numbers.

But the major subject of today's report will be the cruise ship industry, which is on the verge of disappearing.

"Good morning, my fellow Americans. As you probably know by now, I'm Dr. Rebecca Lang, but my friends call me Becca. President Blake has tasked me with the chore of keeping the country up to date with our latest findings about the Pvirus. This morning I'm going to discuss the cruise line industry, a proud, and until now, successful industry. For a long time, cruise ships have had a problem with airborne and surface bacteria. Some have compared a cruise ship to a floating delicatessen, with food served around the clock. It hasn't been uncommon for a ship to become infected and quarantine itself at sea or in a harbor. The Portuguese Virus, or Pvirus, has become a serious problem for the industry, a staggering problem. The other day I mentioned that 75 cruise ships plied the seas from American ports and ports in the Bahamas and the Caribbean. I'm sorry to report that all 75 of the ships have become hit with the Pvirus. Yes, all of them. The worst ship hit, as of this morning, is the *Majesty of the Waves*, a Cunard Lines vessel. As of right now, fully half of the ship's 3,000 passengers and crew have become infected with the virus, and, I'm sorry to say, 560 have died. The ship is quarantined off Bermuda. Cruise lines have simply stopped booking cruises and await further research and study. If you have a cruise booked, I suggest you contact the cruise line to see what arrangements you can make.

"I once again remind you that there are steps we can all take to lessen the dangers of the virus: wear a facemask; socially distance yourself by keeping at least six feet from another person; wash your hands with soap and water any chance you get; stay where you are unless it's absolutely necessary for you to leave home.

"It's no cliché to say that we're all in this together. God bless you, my fellow Americans. We'll speak again tomorrow."

Seth disconnected me from the live feed at 9:45. As usual, my "gang" gave me a round of applause and Jack hugged me. Both Jack and I agree that our little "family" our *Bayfront Gang* is a gift from heaven. They not only get a fantastic job done, they're great people to be with. Seth and Sandy put on their bathing suits and grabbed a couple of inner tubes from the garage. I always wondered what the tubes were for, having been left by the prior owners. Seth figured it out. They're for clamming. If you put a bushel basket in the tube you have a great way to harvest clams while standing in water up to your waist. Just as with the inner tubes, I had always wondered why those bushel baskets were hanging in the garage. For tonight's feast Jack planned linguine and clam sauce, with fresh clams harvested by Seth and Sandy. At Jack's request, Seth stocked up on all sorts of pastas on his trips to the market. I definitely planned on hitting the running track later.

When Sandy and Seth returned with their clam harvest for tonight's dinner, we all sat down to my regular post-White House-report breakfast. Sandy, every bit as good a cook as Jack, prepared a feast of scrambled eggs with sides of chicken, sausages, and sliced potatoes. After we finished and put the dishes in the dishwasher, we sat down for my daily *Bayfront* report. Jack and I had decided that we would keep everybody completely up to date on what's happening, and not just from my White House briefings. Jack and I had decided that the gang would be 100 percent up to date, without any FBI "need to know" bullshit. I told them about Jack's thinking that enzymes may have something to do with our hunt for the end of the killer virus, describing in detail just what an enzyme is. Professor Randy thought the idea was compelling, as did Professor Molly. Although neither of them are scientists, their combined IQs grasped the significance immediately, as did Seth and Sandy. Nice to have a group of really smart people in my gang. I told them about my conversation with Dr. Jenny Clarke from the CDC, and how she was excited about the idea and planned to turn her bright CDC scientists loose on the idea. When Jack and I told them that Jenny was married to our old military boss from Afghanistan, they got a big kick out of the story.

One thing that happened this morning totally bummed me out. My plastic Cracker Jacks engagement ring finally bit the bullet after my constant hand washing. I could glue it back together, but I was sure it wouldn't hold. Seth, God bless him, designed a beautiful frame covered with satin. He fashioned the ring onto a long chain and mounted it in the middle of the frame. He hung it over the fireplace in the den. So, I can still look at my proudest possession, just not on my finger.

———————

That afternoon, in the middle of our Monopoly Tournament, the phone rang and Molly picked it up.

"It's Dr. Jenny Clarke for you and Jack, Becca. She sounds really excited about something." The look on Molly's face echoed Jenny's excitement.

I put the phone on speaker. It was a Facetime call, so we could see her on our computer screen. Although Jenny is a government scientist and likes to keep things secure and secret, I had convinced her that I would keep nothing from *The Bayfront Gang*.

"God bless Jack for his enzyme idea," Jenny shouted. "I've hooked up his idea with our secret weapon."

"Secret weapon?" we all said at once.

"Yes. Her name is Naomi Brinkman, probably our most brilliant scientist."

"Why can't we see her?" I asked.

"Well, I'm in Washington and she's in Atlanta. I could hook you up with a live feed, but she doesn't like to be seen in public anyway."

"Is she shy?" Jack asked.

"You can say that. I'll be frank with you folks, Naomi is on the spectrum. Yes, she's autistic. As is common with many autistic people, she shuns the public. But there is nothing shy about her scientific brain. I'll ask her to join us on the phone from Atlanta, but you will only hear her voice. She can see you, but you can't see her. Here's a photo of her."

Jenny showed us a photo of an extremely thin young woman with a pleasant face, but otherwise nondescript. Jenny then introduced each of us, asking us to raise our hands when called upon. When she introduced Jack, Naomi said, "Jack Parker, Jack Parker, Jack Parker, the handsomest man in the world, world, world." We all cracked up while I stroked Jack's face. "Please don't touch handsome Jack Parker, don't touch, don't touch, don't touch."

I scribbled a note to Jack. "Looks like you've got a big fan in Atlanta."

We all bit our lips while Jenny put Naomi through a polite interrogation. Naomi launched into a long detailed scientific explanation of her findings.

"And what is your conclusion, Naomi?" Jenny asked.

"The virus comes from Yemen, Yemen, Yemen. That's also where they make the enzyme Delta 560, 560, 560."

"Our intelligence so far has indicated that the virus originates in Yemen, but what makes you so sure, Naomi?"

"Yes, yes, yes, in Sana'a, Sana'a, Sana'a. That's the capital of Yemen, Yemen, Yemen."

"Please explain how you came to that conclusion, Naomi," Jenny said.

Naomi explained in scientific detail how she concluded the virus comes from Yemen. I was recording the call, which was good because it was hard to keep up with the brilliant Naomi. She has a confusing speech pattern, and constantly repeats words. That made it especially hard for us to understand her explanation of the science.

"And can you explain why none of the citizens have come down with the virus?" Jenny said, stealing the words from my mouth. I recalled that Buster from the CIA made that observation. Obviously, Buster talks to the CDC people all the time. Naomi's response shocked the hell out of all of us, a happy shock.

"Vaccine, Vaccine, Vaccine," Naomi said. "Yes, they found a cure, cure, cure."

Chapter 49

This is Doctor Lang calling for the Director."

"Hi, Becca, I've been expecting your call," Buster said.

"Buster, I'm sitting here with my gang, and we've just had our minds blown. Jenny said that you just found out like us. My God, not only do they make the virus there, they have a vaccine and an antidote. Looks like your hunch about Yemen was on target."

"Yes, it was. If the President ever asks me for a recommendation on an excellent nuclear test target site facility, I know just the place."

"I hope I'm not overstepping my bounds when I ask what is the next move."

"I'm going to send some of my people to *have a talk* with the leaders of this plot. I'll keep you posted."

After we got off the phone with Buster, Jack and I explained to the gang what he meant by a "talk."

"When Buster says his people will *have a talk,* both Jack and I know what he means. A *talk* means that some bad actors are about to die. That's why we don't ask too many questions when around Buster. He knows things that we have no desire to know. When Buster says he 'takes no shit,' he means it."

Chapter 50

ood evening ladies and gentlemen and welcome to
Special Report. I'm your *Fox News* host, Bret Baier.
We have just received word about a clandestine CIA
operation in Sana'a, the capital of Yemen. CIA operations
are usually secretive, but this incident was so critical that a
full battalion of the 82nd Airborne Division was there to lend
assistance."

Buster's "talk" with the jihadis, aided by the 82nd Airborne
Division, obviously did the job. Of course, Bret Baier wasn't
informed about Buster's "talks."

"They raided the offices of a group believed to be
responsible for the Portuguese Virus, also known as the
Pvirus. The raiding party found hundreds of canisters
containing the virus, but perhaps most important, they found
a vaccine. The distribution around the world of the vaccine
will be conducted under the orders of Dr. Rebecca Lang, the
U.S. director of the war against the virus. Dr. Lang is well-
known as the world's expert on epidemics and pandemics.

"We have with us on the phone, Dr. Lang herself, speaking
to us from her office on Long Island. (I was happy that he
didn't mention that my "office" is a waterfront mansion).

Dr. Lang, please give us your take on this amazing turn of events."

"Thanks for having me on your show, Bret. Just to clarify what you said, the actual distribution of the vaccines will be done under the auspices of the Centers for Disease Control and Prevention, the CDC, in Atlanta. This is the most exciting news possible, Bret. Not only will the world be free of the terrible scourge of the Pvirus, but we now have not only a vaccine to prevent future infections, but the vaccine can be used to cure someone who has become infected. President Blake had asked me to be the point person on communicating to the nation about this horrible disease, and I hope I haven't bored your listeners to death with my daily report of the horrors, but now I will have some good news to report.

"The suspicion that the disease was helped to spread by an enzyme is because of one man, whom I often call the smartest man in the world, my wonderful husband Jack Parker, FBI Agent. Working on his idea, a brilliant scientist at the CDC came up with the scientific details that led to Sana'a, Yemen. I've been asked not to divulge the name of that scientist (Naomi). I'm asking anyone listening to please take a deep breath and remain calm. The distribution of the vaccine will be conducted under the able hands of the CDC. It will be a vast and complex operation, so please be patient. President Blake has asked me to continue to be the spokesperson on this matter, so you will be hearing more from me."

"So, there you have it, ladies and gentlemen, great news from one of our nation's smartest physicians. The war against the virus isn't over, but at least the end is in sight, thanks in no small part to Doctor Lang and her brilliant husband, Jack.

Doctor Lang will be keeping us up to date in the future. Bret Baier signing off for *Fox News*."

My God, our worldwide horror is almost over. *The Bayfront Gang* will have a party tonight.

Epilogue

Six Months Later

Because we had available a life-saving vaccine for the Pvirus, the economy opened up a lot faster than we originally would have hoped for. Three of the nation's largest pharmaceutical companies offered to help in production and distribution of the drugs at their cost, which I found amazing and inspiring. It was also pretty good public relations. My friends at the CDC did a fabulous job overseeing the complex task of distributing the drugs and worked closely with the big three drug companies.

The country and the world began to return to normal. The deaths, including death by suicide, had been staggering, rivaling the Black Plague of the Middle Ages.

To gain access to a restaurant, all a customer needs to do is show a card which indicated that the person had taken the vaccine. I was delighted that these people whom I had put out of work were now back to being employed. The same rule applied to any business that catered to the public.

The stock market took off like a rocket, and Jack's day-trading brain went along for the ride. Thanks to Jack, and the market, our portfolio swelled as never before.

The Bayfront Gang is still together. After we got the good news, Randy Jones, always the delightful wise guy, said, "I've been wondering when the hell Molly and I could leave this gorgeous waterfront estate." Jack and I told him they were more than welcome to stay, especially because we had been working on a book together with him and Molly. Both he and Molly resumed their jobs as college professors, and insisted on paying us a substantial rent, even though we didn't request it. They love their waterfront suite. Seth and Sandy, of course, continued their chores at *Bayfront*. Seth, after consulting with Jack and me, decided to renovate our already beautiful den, as he wrote one song after another. Sandy worked on her latest novel. It will be a love story, not a terrorist thriller. My BFF Rachel and her husband, Mike, come to visit us regularly and often stay over.

I continued my White House press briefings, which were no longer a horror show. I would update the nation on the distribution of the antivirus drugs. Boring as hell, but somehow a nice kind of boring. My White House briefings now consisted of a steady stream of good news.

We had just finished dinner when Jack grabbed me in a hug.

"Becca, my shoulder hurts," Jack said as he kissed me on the neck. It was his private code for telling me he wants to make love. His 'hurt shoulder" was reminiscent of our wonderful budding love affair in Afghanistan.

"Hey, Captain Jack, are you flirting with me?"

"Yes, I am. Maybe we should change the title of our book from *The Love We Almost Lost to The Love We'll Never Lose*. Hell, over the years my flirting has gotten us to a pretty nice place,

I think you'll agree."

"I definitely agree. Keep up with the flirting, Captain."

He took me by the hand, and we went to our bedroom, where I took good care of his "shoulder."

Characters -*The Love We Almost Lost*

Bellamy, Ellen – TV talk show host and Rick's wife

Bellamy, Rick – FBI Agent, head of the Counterterrorism Task Force

Bixby, Tom – Editor, Random House

Blake, Matt – President of the United States

Brinkman, Naomi – CDC scientist

Buster – CIA Director

Clarke, Harry – Lt. Colonel, base commander in Bagram, Afghanistan

Clarke, Jennifer – CDC scientist, and later, Harry's wife

Drake, Miles – FBI safe house supervisor

Franken, Walter – Admiral, Chief of Naval Operations

Franklin, Roger – Building superintendent with assigned name

Jones, Randy – Professor, Terrorism Expert

Lake, Monica – Editor, Random House

Lang, Bob – Private investigator, Becca's uncle

Lang, Mildred – Becca's mother

Lang, Rebecca – Becca - Navy Doctor, Jack Parker's physician

Lang, Troy – Becca's father

Lighthouse, Seth – Handyman and scholar

Lighthouse, Sandra – Seth's's wife and IT expert

Longworth, Carol – FBI Agent, Rick Bellamy's assistant

Maxwell, Bob – Witness Protection Program guest

Maxwell, Grace - Witness Protection Program guest and Bob's wife

Parker, Jack – Captain, US Marine Corps

Parker, Rachel – Jack's sister

Parker, Thomas – Jack's father

Parker, Jane – Jack's mother

Pearson, Molly – Becca and Jack's neighbor

Smith, Mike – NYPD Detective, Jack's friend and neighbor

Smith, Nancy – Mike's wife and insurance investigator

Watson, Sarah – FBI Director

THE BOOKS OF RUSS MORAN

I hope you enjoyed reading *The Love We Almost Lost* as much as I enjoyed writing it.

This book, as well as all my books are available on Amazon. com, and also as ebooks on The Kindle or a Kindle app on your smartphone or iPad.

The Gray Ship – **Book One of** *The Time Magnet Series*
http://amzn.to/16GPumH

A number one Amazon best seller. "This provocative, intensely powerful novel is a must-read for sci-fi fans and Civil War aficionados, though mainstream fiction readers will find it heart-rending and inspiring as well. A rare read that's not only *wildly entertaining, but also profoundly moving.*" — Kirkus Reviews

The Thanksgiving Gang – **Book Two of** *The Time Magnet Series* http://amzn.to/1NzBs7N

The Sequel to *The Gray Ship*. A story of time travel.

"I had never read a book before written in an efficient, minimalistic prose. Instead of writing what most readers want to read, he gives voice to life-like characters, with their flaws and prejudices. They are not infallible superheroes. It's always nice to find a new voice in fiction and to enjoy creativity at its best." — C. Ludewig.

"Breakneck pacing and virtually nonstop action" – Kirkus Reviews

A Time of Fear – **Book Three** of *The Time Magnet Series*
http://amzn.to/1zdjaG9

In a month, five American cities will be devastated by suitcase nuclear bombs.

The time travelers take on their old name, *The Thanksgiving Gang*.

- They know what will happen, because they travelled to the future.

- They know what the result will be. They've seen the devastation.

- They know the details. Five American Cities targeted by nuclear suitcase bombs.

- BUT they don't know where the bombs are—and they don't know how to find them.

The clock is ticking, and millions will soon lose their lives – unless they find the bombs.

"His story is fascinating, and adds even more depth to this already cavernously deep novel. Amazingly unique, chilling and well written, Moran weaves a future that is both desperate and hopeful. Blending modern fears with science fiction results in a tale that will keep you reading long into the night. Five stars!" —Heather

The Skies of Time – **Book Four** of *The Time Magnet Series*
http://amzn.to/1CCC3jg

In *The Skies of Time*, you will recognize the two main characters, Ashley Patterson, now an admiral, and her husband, Jack Thurber. They met and fell in love in *The Gray Ship*, and now they're in for the adventure of their lives in *The Skies of Time*. Ashley and Jack have been such prominent characters in all four books of The Time Magnet Series that I feel like they're old friends. You will also recognize some of the other characters. But if I told you who they are, it would ruin the fun.

"I'm big fan of this series and this one may be the best. I hope there is another book to this series since it keeps getting better. There are a few questions I have about certain events that makes the next one even more suspenseful. These are great books to binge read one after the other." — Time Travel Fan

The Shadows of Terror – Book One of the *Patterns Series*
http://amzn.to/1IDQzJS

A stunning page turner. A novel that explodes off the front page of your newspaper.

Terrorism has a new face, a face that's obscured in the shadows. The radical forces of destruction have learned to make themselves invisible to the West, and preventing a terrorist attack has become almost impossible.

A new war has begun, World War III.

Rick Bellamy, an FBI agent who specializes in counterterrorism, is engaged in his own war, a war with no end.

Bellamy's wife, Ellen, a prominent architect, discovers that she's in the middle of the greatest terror plot to date.

To defeat the enemy, Bellamy first has to uncover the clues, to shine a light on the shadows. He has to find patterns – before it's too late.

"Move over James Patterson and Mary Higgins Clark. There's

a new guy in town. Russ Moran's new book – *The Shadows of Terror*." — Frank O.

The Scent of Revenge - **Book Two in the** *Patterns Series.*
http://amzn.to/1UvDRmw

The world is at war with the forces of terror. FBI Agent Rick Bellamy and his wife, Ellen, find themselves in the middle of a sinister terrorist plot.

Someone is attacking young prominent women, inflicting a horrible disease.

Nobody knows its origin, nobody knows how to stop it, nobody knows how to cure it.

Rick Bellamy and a team of scientists want to go on the offense. But how?

Will the lives of the women be changed forever? When will the attacks stop?

"Heart pounding, can't put down thriller that will force you to look at terrorism in different light. Life in America will never be the same." – Cold Coffee Cafe

Sideswiped-Book One in the Matt Blake series of legal thrillers.
http://amzn.to/1MkxX35

Trial lawyer Matt Blake took on a perfect case.

It involved a sideswipe collision in which his client's husband, an investigative reporter, was killed. The evidence of negligence was overwhelming. Eyewitnesses testified that defendant was talking on his cell phone when he hit the other car.

But was it negligence? Was it an accident?

Or was it murder?

Matt uncovers evidence that the act may have been intentional. Somebody wanted the man silenced. Somebody wanted the man dead.

Somebody had a lot to hide.

The signs started to point to the highest levels of government.

An open-and-shut personal injury case suddenly became a vast conspiracy of terror.

"This book hooks you in from the first line. *Sideswiped* draws you into the world of Matt Blake and you become emotionally attached to him and his journey. The story itself is so well-written and moves quickly. There is never a dull moment." —Sarah Elle

"Moran demonstrates the depth of his writing talent by developing a new genre with *Sideswiped,* a legal thriller. Branching out from his previous novels dealing with time travel, Moran goes in a whole new direction with Book One in the Matt Blake series. He creates a wild but totally believable story of modern day intrigue and suspense. Moran also deftly weaves into this book some of my favorite characters from his prior novels. I am looking forward to starting Book #2 - *The Reformers* — Frank from Lynbrook on August 16, 2016

The Reformers - **Book Two of the Matt Blake Series of legal thrillers, is the sequel to *Sideswiped*.**
http://amzn.to/2m8uMdu

The forces of radical Islam are on the run.

Their leadership has been decimated, their ranks thinned, their power disappearing by the week.

Their recruiting efforts have been cut off, the radical websites shut down, and the attraction of jihad is losing its appeal among the young.

With targeted assassinations, military strikes, as well as the loss of oil fields and gold mines, radical Islam is fast losing power.

But who is responsible?

It isn't the United States Government. It's a new force the world has never seen before.

Lawyer Matt Blake and his wife Diana find themselves in the middle of the most gigantic plot the world has ever seen, a conspiracy that's only begun to grow.

"I've been a fan of the author, Russell Moran, since reading *Sideswiped* a few months ago, so I admittedly went into this book with quite high expectations. That being said, I had no idea that "*The Reformers*" was going to play out in the way that it does and I can see myself giving this book a re-read in the future. In fact, I am even more impressed by the storyline of this read than the last and it has left me excited to see more." Lucidity.

The Keepers of Time – **Book Five of the Time Magnet Series**
http://amzn.to/2wjVSTt

Admiral Ashley Patterson and her husband Jack have done it again. They've traveled through time, 200 years into the future—aboard a nuclear aircraft carrier, Ashley's flagship.

They discover a new world, a strange new world—a post-nuclear war world—one that is both a beacon of hope, and a cry of despair.

They meet a group of people who call themselves *The Keepers of Time,* an organization dedicated to preserving history and culture amid the horrors of a dystopian future.

The world around them has harkened back to a primitive and savage past, one that includes human sacrifice.

Ashley knows they must have to get back to the present to warn the government of the unspeakable horrors that await. But finding the way back to the present is their greatest challenge, an almost insurmountable one.

"The Keepers of Time is a really interesting take on current geopolitical events and where they are leading. From reading previous books in the series, the cast of characters is as familiar as the people next door and it was great to reconnect with them. Moran's legal background illuminates what happens when our legal structure disappears, and he has zeroed in on an essential thing about civilization -- records of the past. A great read!" Robert Shearer

"<u>Time flies when you're scared out of your mind</u>. The author's superb writing skills will quickly draw you into the story. Forty-two fast paced chapters will keep turning the pages of this novel until the end. Well-developed cast of realistic characters that you will relate to one will keep you engaged. One of my favorite things about Moran's books is his entire cast of characters detailed in the back of the book. I admit to reading about the cast first in order to firmly get everyone in my mind. As a follower of his, I know each character is important to the plot and I don't want to miss anything or overlook anyone." Cold Coffee

"A wild time travel yarn that starts fast and doesn't slow down until the end."

A Reunion in Time
http://amzn.to/2tneIsg

What if a 37-year-old adult travels back 20 years in time and finds himself in high school, followed by his 36-year-old wife? They're now teenagers, 17 and 16.

Adults in teenage bodies, they struggle to convince the people from their past that they are real, not apparitions. With the benefit of hindsight, they know the history of the past 20 years, and it isn't pretty.

Rick and Ellen are married, and now have to adjust to married life as teenagers in 2001. Rick is a senior FBI official and Ellen is a famous architect.

But everybody sees them as kids. Nobody believes that they're married, and nobody believes their stories—until Rick and Ellen predict 9/11.

How do they find their way back to the year they came from? How do they warn the authorities of the cataclysm that will occur in the future? The answer is to find the time portal—the wormhole—that brought them to 2001. But the site has changed. It's no longer the place where they crossed the wormhole. Will they live out the balance of their lives beginning as teenagers?

"We've all wished we could go back to earlier times with the mind we have now. This Russell Moran book takes you there and it is a fun creative romp well worth reading. *A Reunion in Time* is highly recommend!" Kindle Customer.

The President is Missing – Book Three of the Matt Blake series.
http://amzn.to/2t9v7wu

While he was addressing the nation from a submerged nuclear submarine, President Blake's message is suddenly cut off. Anyone listening heard an explosion. The explosion was followed by floating debris five minutes later.

First Lady Dee Blake has doubts, which she shares with naval high command and the new president. She thinks the explosion and the debris were a ruse to make people think the sub was destroyed, and her husband with it.

Could the sub have been hijacked and the president kidnapped?

But who would commit such an act? What is its purpose?

Was it Russia, China, Iran, or a shadowy group of freelance terrorists?

The new president appoints Dee as his Chief of Staff, with explicit instructions to find the missing submarine—and President Matt Blake.

Her life, and the life of the nation, suddenly take a horrifying turn.

"Russ Moran wrote a true thriller, with a strong plot and even stronger characters. To think that there are good guys - Russian Naval Admirals, no less - made this book not only a solid who-done-it but also a strong 'why did they do it?' " Unka Heshie

Robot Depot
http://amzn.to/2zXW7C2

Mike Bateman is a visionary businessman, the creator and CEO of the fabulously successful chain of stores, Robot Depot, a company dedicated to selling robots and Artificial Intelligence machines for a variety of uses.

The company is a darling of Wall Street and is the most popular destination for consumers and businesses looking for labor saving devices.

But the company caught the eye of ISIS, the terrorist Islamic State. They discover a great way to deliver bombs – using the products of Robot Depot to kill people.

Robot Depot changed from being a popular company to an object of fear because of the tampered products it sells. The terrorists use the company for "terror spectaculars," including the destruction of a skyscraper, a drone attack on Yankee Stadium, and the bombing of a children's sailing regatta.

Mike Bateman and the FBI are in a race to stop his products from becoming weapons, a race to stop the wanton killings. His wife and partner, Jenny, discovers the true meaning of terror one horrible summer day.

"Moran just got a new fan. This is the first book of Moran's that I've read, but I look forward to reading more of his work. I enjoyed this story, and found that Moran is not only a good writer, but he's a good storyteller as well. It's an interesting and creative story, mixing new technology and AI uses, with terrorism. It's a thriller that keeps the reader turning the page, and it's extremely captivating. I enjoyed the story and look forward to future works of his." Amy's Bookshelf

A Climate of Doubt
https://amzn.to/2OSwcHR

Forget what you ever heard about climate change.

Forget your preconceived notions about reality itself.

Instantly, you are in a new world, a horrifying world, a world you don't understand.

On a hot summer day, Homeland Security Secretary, Rick Bellamy, and his wife Ellen, a famous TV talk show host, walked along the ocean front trying to escape the heat. Suddenly the temperature dropped from the high 90s to below freezing in a matter of minutes. It began to snow—*on July 16.*

The temperatures across the country and the world plummeted, creating winter in summer.

Bellamy and the rest of the government struggled to cope with the suddenly new climate, but to cope, they first had to find out what happened.

Scientists from academia blamed the weather on a sudden acceleration of climate change, but they were unable to explain a 60-degree temperature drop in a matter of minutes.

Two astronauts in an American space station realized that the sudden weather calamity coincided with a test of the 20 satellites that the space station controlled.

Attention focused on a huge American corporation that owned the space station and the satellites. Could there be a connection between the satellite tests and the radical drop in temperature?

As the deaths piled up and the world economy tilted toward disaster because of gigantic summer blizzards, Rick Bellamy and his team struggled to find answers before it was too late. Was it a sudden shift in climate change or did it have something to do with the satellites? The biggest question remained—was the catastrophe an accident, or was somebody controlling the weather? Was it terror?

Bundle up and get this page-turning thriller. You're in for a wild ride. The book was published in May of 2018. It's Book Four of the Matt Blake Series. Matt and Dee Blake take on their biggest challenge to date, along with our old friends, Rick and Ellen Bellamy.

"Mr. Moran does a masterful job of crafting an action-packed, suspenseful read about the devastating consequences of climate manipulation. The diabolical mastermind behind the caper is a dictator of the worst kind—a man without conscience who cares only for power. Through the magic of Mr. Moran's digital pen, the men and woman in white hats are three-dimensional and vividly real. While this is a work of fiction, it's plausible fiction. We can easily relate to the horrific consequences of such an act of terrorism as so capably portrayed in Mr. Moran's prose." – Colorado Avid Reader

The Maltese Incident – A Story of Time Travel - **Book One of the Harry and Meg Series,** the prequel to *The Violent Sea.* https://amzn.to/2RclZCT

You're on a beautiful cruise ship.

The April sky is full of stars.

Suddenly, the ship rumbles, and instantly the stars disappear.

"What the hell was that?" Captain Fenton yelled.

"Beats me, captain. I've never seen anything like it," the first officer said.

They would soon discover that the ship, *The Maltese*, had just traveled through time—millions of years to the past.

The captain, Harry Fenton, a highly decorated naval war hero, realizes the greatest battle of his life lay ahead of him.

Captain Harry, a widow, falls in love with a beautiful passenger, Meg Johnson, an executive with the company that owns the ship.

After a whirlwind romance, they marry—in the ship's ballroom—100 million years in the past.

Captain Harry convinces the passengers and crew that they must move ashore to a tropical island because the ship is running out of fuel and supplies. He organizes a group to go ashore and inspect the island.

An ancient forest inhabited by dinosaurs awaits them.

Meg wants to go with them. Harry, fearing for her safety, tries to convince her to stay on the ship.

Meg demonstrates that she is proficient with a gun by taking apart a rifle and reassembling it—in 15 seconds. Harry marvels that he's never seen such an expert gun handler—or accurate shooter. So, AR-15 in hand, Meg joins the inspection party. Charging dinosaurs are no match for Meg Fenton's firepower.

Will the 1,000 souls ever make it back to the time they came from, or will they remain stranded in the distant past?

A scientist aboard theorizes that, to return to their present time, they need to go back to the time portal, or wormhole, that brought them to the past.

But the ship doesn't have enough fuel for the journey.

Realizing that their lives have hit the reset button, the crew and passengers construct a community in the forest—Malta Town.

Under Harry and Meg's leadership, they create a court system, a legislature, and all the elements of a small budding democracy. Meg figures out a way to harness hydroelectric power from a nearby waterfall. Everybody thinks of Harry and Meg as the heart and soul of Malta Town. They begin their new lives—among the dinosaurs.

The Maltese Incident is a riveting tale of time travel, love, courage, and horror.

Get this page turner now and prepare for the ride of your life.

"As with Moran's work, he continues to be a great storyteller. I recommend reading this from title to end. It's well written, and filled with intensity and levity." Amy's Bookshelf

The Violent Sea – A Story of Time Travel - **Book Two of the Harry and Meg Series,** the sequel to *The Maltese Incident.* https://amzn.to/2AT5ypI

The Violent Sea is a novel of war, time travel, military history. It's the second book in the Harry and Meg Series. It's also a sweet romance between Harry and his wife, Meg.

Rear Admiral Harry Fenton has done it again. He's traveled through time to a different era. He finds himself, with a serious head injury from a fall, at Pearl Harbor Base Hospital on May 16, 1942, three weeks before the Battle of Midway. His wife and aide, Lieutenant Meg Fenton, is worried sick, and waits for him—in 2018.

Admiral Harry is the commanding officer of Carrier Strike Group 14 in 2018, but the people in 1942 think he's a busted-up hallucinating sailor who imagines himself an admiral.

Admiral Raymond Spruance is commanding officer of Carrier Task Force 16. After hearing about Harry's time travel stories, Spruance orders him brought to his flagship, the *USS Enterprise*. After Harry tells him about his time travel experiences, Spruance is convinced the man is insane.

But after speaking to him at length, Spruance is amazed at Harry's knowledge of naval tactics and strategy. He calls Harry's bluff and orders him to stay aboard the *Enterprise* for her upcoming engagement at the Battle of Midway.

By the end of the battle, Spruance is convinced Harry is an admiral, and thinks of him as a friend.

Now Harry needs to figure out how to travel back to 2018, to his carrier command, but most importantly, to the love of his life, Lieutenant Meg.

After Harry returns to the present, the Fentons are deployed on Harry's flagship, the *USS Gerald R. Ford*. The ship encounters another wormhole, this one in the ocean. They are transported to1944 and participate in the Battle of Leyte Gulf.

The book took me 10 months to write. It went through 20 drafts and three rounds with my editors. I did copious research for the book to ensure its historical accuracy. If you enjoy the genre of time travel, I think you will love this book. I got to know my two main characters in the prequel, *The Maltese Incident*. Harry and Meg are deeply in love but enjoy constant banter and wisecracks. One of my favorite characters, Admiral Ashley Patterson of *The Gray Ship*, makes an important cameo appearance in *The Violent Sea*.

"What a great book. You will love this book. Time travel telling at its best. At the end you will believe it is possible. Russell Moran has crafted a great continuation from *The Maltese Incident* his character development has continued from the first book thru out this book and possibly beyond. His writing is so detail oriented you will find yourself believing that time travel is not only real but possible. This book was given to me as a gift but it turned out to be one of the greatest gifts I have ever received. You will find that your investment of money and time reading this book to be a great investment. Time and money both well spent." Mike the Mailman

A Sea of Fear – A Novel of Time Travel - Book 3 of The Harry and Meg Series.
https://amzn.to/2GERuSx

You're Five-Star Admiral Harry Fenton, whom President Blake calls the greatest fighting admiral in American history.

Along with your Navy Commander wife, Meg, you lead your carrier strike group against the worst enemy the country has faced since World War II, a small nation that is intent on destroying the world's shipping industry. The seas of the world have become scenes of plunder, pillage, and mass murder.

The president has convinced you to come out of retirement and put an end to the looming crisis. He promotes you to Fleet Admiral, the highest-ranking officer since Admiral Chester Nimitz.

You and Meg were having a pleasant retirement, running a world-class resort that you bought in Rhode Island. But when the president pleads you to "Give 'em Hell, Harry," you know that you can't ignore his call to duty.

As people who have time traveled in the past, you come up with an idea to travel three years into the future. With President Blake's blessing, you and Meg lead a group of officers into the future. What you find is horrifying, an America taken over by a totalitarian dictator.

You return to the past and report your findings. President Blake, hearing your terrifying story, convinces you that you have an even bigger call to duty, the greatest challenge of your life. You take on the challenge for one reason—Meg will be at your side.

As in the first two books of the Harry and Meg Series, *The Maltese Incident* and *The Violent Sea*, *A Sea of Fear* is a sweet romance between two of literature's most exciting and likable characters, Harry and Meg Fenton.

A Sea of Fear is a story of war, politics, time travel, and love.

"This story is incredible. I felt like it was real-life and happening NOW! The way the political world is unfolding with the lies and innuendos, something like this could be possible. The main couple, husband and wife, Meg and Harry worked together to solve and help the nation climb onto its rock-solid feet. Surely this is the integrity that the United States government stands for. They had me in their corner wanting to see them win against the evil Antonio Martin. Read the story, it will enthrall and pull you in as it did me... Great ending." Cristella

Leonardo Murphy – A Coming of Age Thriller
https://amzn.to/31vzC4S

You just launched a satellite into space without a rocket.

You invented a computer algorithm that writes novels.

You just entered Harvard University on a full scholarship after completing high school in two years.

Not bad for a 12-year-old kid.

Leonardo changed his name from William to Leonardo to honor his hero, Leonardo da Vinci. Young Leonardo Murphy has the second highest IQ ever recorded.

Leonardo, now 25, met a beautiful young woman named Janice, and fell madly in love. They married a year later.

Janice and Leonardo, who she calls "Lee," collaborate on various projects with the CIA and FBI.

But their intelligence activities put a target on their backs. They narrowly escape four assassination attempts.

Leonardo Murphy is a breathtakingly fast coming-of-age thriller about one of the most fascinating characters you will ever meet in literature. Instantly, you are shoulder to shoulder with the world's most amazing genius.

"<u>Finally, a believable super hero comes to life!</u> Peaks and valleys of horrific actions are neatly juxtaposed against comic relief. The humor, ranging between the poles of mild to downright hysterical, will surely tickle your funny bone. The frequent use of the protagonist's favorite word (26 matches found throughout), which I won't divulge, would ordinarily belabor one's prose, save when Leonardo employs the term. As a matter of fact, the story concludes with that very word, but rather endearingly. No, I did not ruin the ending for you folks. You'll see." – Robert Banfelder

The Pineaire Incident – Book 4 of the Harry and Meg Series
https://amzn.to/2VXQ2lp

One hundred gigantic fast submarines suddenly appear in the ocean.

President Harry Fenton and his First Lady, Meg are shocked by the event, as are all the leaders of the world.

Where are the submarines from? What do they want? What are their intentions?

Six Russian submarines attack one of the mystery subs. All six Russian subs are destroyed in two minutes.

President Fenton, along with Meg, reaches out to contact the leader of the strange fleet. They are amazed to discover that the subs are from another planet, Planet Pineaire.

But they're pleased to find out that the Pinearians came in peace, and bring with them an amazing gift, a new type of fuel that can revolutionize life on earth.

Get ready for an interplanetary thrill ride. *The Pinaire Incident* is Book 4 of the Harry and Meg series.

"Right at the beginning, we learn that 100 giant submarines are discovered with no idea how they could all suddenly appear. Being familiar with Harry & Meg, I immediately presumed they must have Time Traveled from some future time. Uh Oh, I almost gave away an important detail. You should already know that Harry and Meg are President and First Lady having recently defeated a small rogue nation that destroyed the Cruise Ship industry and nearly took over the world's Shipping Industry. You might think peaceful times are ahead when abruptly, 100 of these 1,800 foot long submarines appear. Five Stars" – The Holey One

Puzzles Book 1 – A Detective Love Story
https://amzn.to/2MI6TEo

Veteran police detectives Bobbie Nelson and Bob Lawton are partnered. They're both concerned that they may not get along. They're both highly skilled and love their work—They love to solve puzzles. They soon learn that they don't just love their jobs, they love each other. *Puzzles* is an action-packed police thriller wrapped around a sweet romance.

Bobbie and Bob are two of the most exciting and likeable characters you will find in literature.

"This book should be kept out of the hands of crooks, criminals, terrorists, and any others planning to do evil. There are so many techniques utilized by skilled detectives that are revealed that this book could be used as a training guide by the Bad Guys. Even so, the reality is that fundamental police work is what solves most crimes. Gathering and evaluating massive amounts of data and looking for patterns or repeating details is what our two main characters excel at." The Holey One

"Russell Moran has done it again with Puzzles: A Detective Love Story. Each case builds upon earlier ones, with the BBs fine-tuning their puzzle-solving techniques to such a degree it's not long before the FBI and CIA reach out them to piece together more complicated scenarios impacting on society. Russell has created an easy-to-read and fast-paced story, which will keep you turning the pages late into the evening to find out what happens next. I can't wait for the next book in the series!" R. J. Krzak

Puzzles, Book 2 – A Detective Love Story
https://amzn.to/3bmiqEh

The further adventures of Detectives Bob Lawton and Bobbie Nelson, now married. NYPD Detectives First Grade Bobbie Nelson and Bob Layton are partners, husband and wife, and, as Bobbie loves to say, best friends. They both agree that the day they were partnered was the luckiest day of their lives. Police Commissioner Ralph Norquist is their boss and also their good friend. He nicknames them, "the BBs." Norquist discovers that he can assign the most difficult cases to them and they will get the job done. It's almost routine the way they solve child kidnapping cases, serial killer murders, attacks on subway trains, a huge case of drone attacks on football stadiums, and Internet fraud attacks on senior citizens. But what never becomes routine is their love for each other. When they get to their office in the morning, they begin the day with a hug and a kiss. Their partnership almost ended when Bobbie was shot in the head at a crime scene. She spent six long weeks in a semi-comatose state. Bob said it was the worst six weeks of his life, not knowing if Bobbie would fully recover. Fortunately, the bullet wound did no permanent brain damage, and Bobbie came back to her old self, including her photographic memory. Besides being famous detectives, they're also talented writers. Bob had written a best-selling crime novel before they met, and they both collaborated on a nonfiction book on the art of being a detective. That book became a runaway best seller and the royalties poured in. Their book profits, combined with a generous inheritance from Bob's uncle, as well as their combined salaries, made them more than comfortable financially. They renovated their apartment near police headquarters. Bob had bought the building before they met. After a neighboring tenant moved out. They knocked down a wall and created a 3,000 square foot apartment, a three-block walk from One Police

Plaza. Realizing that they need to get away from their hectic work occasionally, they bought a beautiful mansion in East Hampton, and they love to spend weekends there with friends and family—until they discover they are being stalked by a serial killer.

The Long Island Project
https://amzn.to/2WgJC2n

"Another winner!

Our old friends, Detectives Bobbie Nelson and Bob Lawton, "the BBs," are engaged in the most frightening case of their career, an armed quarantine of Long Island by a sinister group. To find the answer to the problem, they travel through time to 1942, and discover the problem is larger than they had thought.

The third novel in Russel's Puzzles series, we meet up again with the infamous detectives, Bobbie Nelson and Bob Lawson as they're called upon to solve another problem. Why is Long Island under quarantine, and who is behind it? Before long, they uncover a conspiracy, which could lead a takeover through mind control and time travel.

"As with all of Moran's novels, the characters adapt to the situations they find themselves in and their interactions bring the best out in the 'good guys and gals' and will turn readers against those behind the conspiracy. There's plenty of intrigue for everyone as the 'BBs' solve their latest puzzle. I look forward to their next adventure!" RK

The Silent Author
https://amzn.to/3cBLRlR

Author Melanie Pierce is widely acknowledged to be the country's greatest novelist. Suddenly she faces the worst form of censorship imaginable – Editorial Terrorism. Her words are no longer her own. Before she can publish a book, she, and her fellow authors, must submit the manuscript to a shadowy group of terrorists. Failure to do so will result in the death of one of her loved ones.

A page-turning thriller about a famous page-turning author. Melanie's husband, Max Wakefield, is an FBI agent, and has been assigned to lead what had become known as The Silent Author Case. His dedication as an FBI agent, as well as his deep love for his wife, Melanie, launched Max into the most dangerous assignment of his career.

"A thrilling plot shifting page turner about a page turning author."

A Charter Through Time
https://amzn.to/34f9BM4

Former federal prosecutor, Janey Drake, has resigned her legal job because she could no longer put up with the stress of prosecuting drug dealers and the frustrating meanderings of the criminal justice system. She decides to resign after an ironclad case was dismissed by a "caring" judge. She takes on a new life that she loves, chartering her 60-foot yacht that was a gift from her wealthy father. An experienced large boat captain, Janey has found a cure for the high stress work of her former occupation.

She also found a cure for her loneliness when she met the man of her dreams by a chance encounter in a diner. Jack Fleming is a famous novelist and loves his work, and soon finds out that he loves Janey, his accidental friend from the diner.

He and Janey fall impossibly in love with each other and found a way to blend their lives—cruising the high seas and writing about it. Janey has taken on the role as Jack's editor and she couldn't be happier.

But suddenly their happy lives together take on a frightening new dimension. While cruising off New London, Connecticut, their boat encounters a wormhole or time portal, and they find themselves two years into the future, a horrifying future that had seen a nuclear war. They find out that their apartment building in Manhattan was the target for one of the bombs. Yes, they discover that they had been killed, two years ago. But yet they're alive. Time travel is a strange phenomenon, and sometimes a scary one.

They realize that they have no choice. They must return to the past and warn the government about the coming horror.

They begin the most terrifying experience of their lives—how to go back in time and prevent your own death, and the deaths of millions of others.

"A time-travel mind bender."

About the Author

In addition to the 23 novels listed here, I have also published five nonfiction books: *Justice in America: How it Works—How it Fails; The APT Principle: The Business Plan That You Carry in Your Head; Boating Basics: The Boattalk Book of Boating Tips; If You're Injured: A Consumer Guide to Personal Injury Law; How to Create More Time.* My latest nonfiction book is *The Novel - A Writer's Guide - Discover the Joy of Writing Fiction* published in November 2018.

I'm a lawyer and a veteran of the United States Navy. I live on Long Island, New York, with my wife and editor, Lynda, a Shih-Tzu named Sammie, and a Golden Retriever named Maggie.

A Personal Request

I hope you enjoyed reading The Love We Almost Lost as much as I enjoyed writing it. Becca and Jack are now two of my favorite characters. I think of them as old friends. You will be seeing more of them in future books.

Please consider leaving a brief review on amazon.com. It doesn't need to be lengthy or elaborate, just your thoughts on the characters, the scenes, and the story. Book reviews are the lifeblood of an author.